HOPE LIES IN LESS

Kris Wehrmeister

Printed in the United States of America

First Printing, 2015

ISBN: 978-0-692-44186-2

Published by Pretty All True
Lake Oswego, Oregon 97034

www.PrettyAllTrue.com

Dear reader —

These stories and the characters contained within their tellings are fictional. If you recognize yourself within this collection, I have either done a brilliant job of creating a world and a moment into which you have projected your identity, or you are yourself a product of my imagination. Either truth is fine.

    — Kris

For my husband, who believes in ... me.

Table of Contents

Hope lies in less ...

Watch

She glances at the dashboard estimate of arrival – another thirty minutes. Staring out the open window, Elena breathes in the late-summer dusk. She loves this particular light; she had commented on it once as they were driving beneath an arch of overhung branches. "It's like everything is more real somehow," and then she had craned her neck to stare up through the windshield. "It's like everything's in 3-D." Which, obviously, wasn't exactly what she'd meant to say, but her point had been lost to mocking laughter.

She stares out into the light, feeling somehow defensive of that one-time observation – it *was* true; the light gives everything a sort of hyper-reality. It's like the moment in a 3-D movie when the effect kicks in, when the spaces you had always known existed become suddenly navigable and dimensional ... yes, that's what she had meant to say. That moment beneath the tree branches – it had felt as though a part of her might float upward and through the levels of limbs. It was the sort of light that made one feel small, small enough to pass through the routes that had always been there. She sighs, realizing this explanation makes her sound insane.

"Something wrong?"

Elena stares straight ahead now, grateful as always to be excused from eye contact. "I worry she won't find her way."

He reaches to pat her knee. "You worry too much. She's going to be fine."

"What if she isn't, though? Going to be fine, I mean. What if she isn't?"

"Listen, she's going to be fine." He removes his hand from her knee, fiddles with the radio. "I never know what you want me to say. She's going to be herself." His voice grows impatient. "I can't figure out if you are scared she will be too much like you or not at all, but it doesn't matter – she's going to be herself and she will find her way."

With her hands clenched in her lap, Elena knows she should let the conversation end there, but she can't help herself. "But what if she doesn't find her way?"

He takes a deep breath. "She will find her way because it's her life and the path she chooses will be hers. There is no wrong ... it's her life."

She wants to punch him.

The car turns and the new road is smaller and empty except for their car and lined with overgrown shrubbery on her side, so close she could reach her arm out the window and run the tips of her fingers along the leaves. She stares ahead and to the side, unfocuses her eyes a bit, allows the green to undulate and ribbon, a muscled hedge of snake. She blinks, and the details come into view ... the light seeping through the gaps to show her the hiding places in the scenery. The light is fading a bit now, but there is still magic, still the possibility of paths revealed.

Perhaps a hundred yards ahead, a small child steps sideways from the hedges. A girl, thin and intent and alone, dressed in dark. The girl stands motionless, arms at her sides, and she stares down the road at them, her left side pressed to the shrubbery. As the car hurtles forward, the child stares as though she is readying herself, coming to a decision.

In the car, Elena senses a coiled tension in the girl's body. She is filled with a panicked certainty the child has been waiting for their arrival. She can feel the impact as though she has already lived it.

They are going to hit the child.

The child is going to take a single step into their path and they are going to hit her.

Elena stiffens helplessly against the future as she cries, "Watch!"

As the last distance between here and there is closed, the small girl turns her head, turns her head so that she is no longer watching the car's approach but instead tracking its progress past her position. With a slight toss of her head, the small girl seems to mock the terror that travels without touching her ... *Look how easy it is to hurt.* Except that's not right, and suddenly the small girl is a deer.

Elena's mind races backward to make sense of what she knows.

A small female deer, only partially stepped from the shrubbery into the arm's length of space between the green and the road, upper body angled and aligned with her front feet, the remainder of her body concealed from view. Her face flattened by a turning to gauge the speed of the only vehicle on the road. Not a child at all. A trick of the light and perception.

Elena meets the deer's eyes for a split-second, large and brown and untroubled.

So close.

She whirls in her seat as they pass to watch the deer step calmly from the shrubbery, walk across the road, and then disappear again.

Not a child.

Elena sinks limply into her seat as the light fades into evening.

He reaches to pat her knee again. "You OK?"

All she can taste is hatred for the small girl's mother.

So she says nothing.

Father

She sits in a darkened room, staring out over the blue patience of her computer screen through the glass that holds the rest of the world apart from the within in which she exists. There is, as there often is with her, a thick gray smudged sort of feeling, as though boundaries are being smeared by unseen hands, followed by the prickle of whispered repeat along the back of her neck – there are no boundaries without agreement, and there is no agreement without other. The outlines she imposes hold the shape of her reality as glass holds the darkness, which is to say ... only until a light appears to cast a shadow ... through.

Into this collapse of worlds, there appear upward-seeking tendrils of pale ... thin solidities of smoke given substance by heat and destruction and toxicity exhaled. Just beyond the liquid glass, just beyond and just below, a cigarette unseen burns, dangled between lips that are her own and have been hers. Twin shadows of pulsed other dance in spiraling upward grace, the velvet smooth of edges fraying with the distance traveled from fuel to diffusion, from there to here.

There is the scent of smoke across the permeables of time and space and truth.

The rough of long-ago abrading sand.

The fire of blue eyes and the small golden jewel of agony.

Glass holds the darkness not at all.

Shadows cast across pane.

Cigarette extinguished.

She exhales.

Into this moment presses a different truth ... the smoke takes shape and alights against the window, a shadow in reverse, a small ghostly figure of pale cream once evanescence.

A moth.

She leans forward to brush careful fingers along the dusty silhouette of here and now.

But she whispers to the other, "Stay."

And so he does.

By agreement.

Petrichor

He walked along the path with his head down, his hands in his pockets. It was warm. There was a slight breeze. It was about to rain. Dressed in jeans and a T-shirt, he was as unprepared for the rain as he was for anything that had not yet happened; the future had stopped mattering some time ago.

A single raindrop hit the nape of his neck and rolled downward along flesh, focusing his attention. More rain fell, as though flung from fingertips, a haphazard scatter of droplets along the ground. He stopped walking and watched as the still-hesitant rain stenciled the world, the shapes of things revealed in their obstruction. Around his feet, a small misshapen circle of dry earth represented all that he was able to prevent. He bent to run a finger along the curved outline as the rain continued to fall and distinctions ran into entirety. His mind wandered, lost in thoughts of absorption and circles of impact and proof of absence. He closed his eyes and raised dampened fingertips to his lips and inhaled deeply of the intrusion on negative space.

"Petrichor."

He looked up. She stood staring at him, and she said again when he said nothing, "Petrichor. The smell of new rain on dusty earth – that's the word for the scent. A harsh sounding word for a beautiful thing, don't you think?"

He stood. The rain kept falling, but it wasn't the sort of rain from which one needed refuge, and so they stood together as it fell. The space he could protect shrank to his footprint on the world. After a few moments' silence, it occurred to him he should say something, and with horror, he heard himself say, "My son is dead."

She nodded, lifted her face to the rain. "A lot of people are."

He nodded as well.

He considered. Generally, when words couldn't be avoided, he told people his son died in a car accident. It was simpler than the truth. Everyone understood about car accidents – a high-velocity crush of flesh and bone against metal and glass. There was little need of explanation beyond the simple statement of occurrence.

He tried to never speak of his son, but when it was unavoidable, he said simply, "My son James was nineteen. He died in a car crash a little over a year ago."

Everyone was sorry. He hated the offerings. It seemed to him the apologies slipped moist and malevolent on overeager exhalation, a bit of airborne toxicity he was then unable to avoid inhaling on his next breath.

Everyone was sorry. Everyone wanted him to know. The world stank with their wanting.

He waited uneasily for her to want.

Instead, all he smelled was rain. She lifted a palm to catch a few drops. "I would go home, but it will stop soon, this rain. You can feel its uncertainty." As if the skies heard her dismissal, the rain tapered off and then ceased altogether. She lifted her face again, this time to sunlight. She smiled. "I told you so."

He inhaled deeply of the scented air. "What did you say the word was?"

"Petrichor. It sounds harsh and military, doesn't it? It's derived from two Greek words." She channeled fingers through damp hair. Her hair was shoulder-length and wavy, a glossy brown streaked with lightning. Her fingers were thin, the pinky on her right hand slightly crooked, as though it had long ago been mis-set after a break. He tried to remember the last time he had noticed the details of anyone beyond his own grief. Her eyes met his; her eyes were a sort of golden gray, the color of tarnished silver. She was about his age, he thought. Freckles danced along the lines of her face as she smiled again. "*Petros*, meaning stone and *ichor*, the golden blood of the gods. Blood against stone."

"I've never heard that word."

She shrugged. "It's enough that you have breathed it."

Stepping out of the spots they held, they fell into step together, and they walked along the path as though they had agreed on a destination. He wondered from what journey he had detoured her; she was dressed to go running, but she seemed content to walk beside him. He waited for her to speak, and when she did not, he found, for the first time in a very long time, that he wanted to listen, and so he asked, "Are there things you would say?"

She glanced at him without slowing her steps. "Of course."

"Tell me."

She said nothing at first, gathering her thoughts, and then she began. "When I was very young, we lived in Chicago. I recall trips to various museums, my favorite being *The Art Institute*. It was an enormous stone building with wide stone steps flanked on either side by huge green lions." She looked at him, explaining, "The lions were bronze, greened by exposure to the elements." Satisfied that he understood, she continued, "The lions weren't identical. They were posed differently, and I remember they were named for their poses – the first of defiance and the second of prowl."

"Defiance and Prowl?"

"Yes, I don't know if they had actual names, those lions, but that's how I was introduced to them. That's how I knew them."

He thought back, realized he hadn't offered his own name. "My name is Jeremy, by the way. Go on."

She nodded acknowledgment. "My name is Sophie. It's funny, the things one remembers and the things that slip away. I remember the lions. I remember the building itself. I remember the hallways and the shapes of paintings and sculptures in the space, but I remember only one painting in detail. Even though I visited the museum several times, I remember only one painting."

"Not so strange. How old were you?"

"Six ... perhaps seven years old."

"Which painting has stayed with you?"

Her voice grew dreamy. "It was an enormous painting, as big as the wall of my bedroom at home. The painting was ostensibly of people relaxing in a park by the water, but everyone was so stiff and formal looking; it looked nothing like any relaxing I had ever seen. The women carried parasols and wore old-fashioned dresses with tiny waists and long bustled skirts. There was a man lying in the grass wearing a top-hat. There was a woman with a monkey on a leash, which I thought was very silly. From the middle of the painting, a small sunlit girl appeared to stare out at the viewer, and it was explained to me that the artist intended the girl to communicate a disdainful message of judgment for the scene around her, that the painting was meant to be understood as an indictment of Paris' leisure class."

"Do you remember the name of the painting?"

"Yes, of course. The artist is Georges Seurat. The painting is called *A Sunday on La Grande Jatte* ... a painting done in tiny dots of saturated color."

"Pointillism."

"Yes!" She was pleased he knew. "I was so impressed as a child with how the artist created a world out of pinpoints of color. It was like a magic trick; the eye was fooled into seeing only the entirety instead of the infinitesimal bits of the making."

"Like the rain," he thought aloud.

"The rain?"

He explained, "The rain falls in a million tiny bits to create the artistry that is the drenching. Earlier, I was watching as the first drops fell, noticing how some spaces are filled and some are left, creating a version of the truth through which the water has fallen. Of course, the rain keeps falling, until eventually everything is just wet, the details lost to the whole."

"That's lovely."

He nodded. "The painting, though ... it's not just the smaller bits of the whole that stayed with you."

She shook her head slowly as they walked. "No. After I had seen the painting on three different visits, I started to have nightmares – terrible dreams in which a faceless child chased me through shadows and darkness. She was dressed in a shapeless bland cloak, and she was too short – oddly truncated, as though she was legless. She wore a red scarf tied around her head and neck, and her face was pale and smooth as a stone. When she moved, she seemed to float or glide, and night after night, she chased me through my sleep."

"Petrichor."

She stopped walking and turned to him, confused. "What?"

He apologized. "I'm sorry. The red scarf against the smooth stone of the child's face – it made me think of what you said – the blood of gods against stone."

Her eyes widened. "I hadn't seen that."

Not wanting her to stop talking, he bowed slightly and extended an arm to invite her along the path. "Go on."

They walked again, and when she spoke, there was a new note of intimacy to the telling, as though she now acknowledged the role he was playing in the words she shared. "When the nightmares continued, it seemed to me they were tied to the painting, as though the girl had stepped from the painting to confront me. I tried to explain to my parents, but they were well acquainted with the painting, and they assured me there was no faceless red-scarfed girl hidden in its imagery. They spoke again of the small girl who stood in sunlight and stared out at the viewer, but I knew the child of my nightmares wasn't her. I could not shake the feeling the girl existed, even if only in points of color, and so I begged my parents to take me to the museum again."

"Did they?"

"Yes, several weeks after the nightmares began, they relented. We stood together before the painting, and I pointed, terrified and triumphant, at the faceless child of my dreams. She was there, off to the left of the little sunlit girl, a small featureless demon." She sighed. "Except, as it turned out, I was seeing what wasn't there. My mother knelt beside me and looked with me until I saw what she saw – a small girl sitting in the grass, her back to the viewer. Her beige cloak was gathered around her body, and on her head she wore a white hat encircled with red ribbon, ribbon which then fell in lengths down her back. What I had imagined a smooth stone face was in fact the top of a hat."

She sank into silence. He thought for a moment that she had arrived at the end of the story, but then she said, "I've been having nightmares lately."

"Of the faceless child?"

"Not exactly, no. In my nightmares, my daughter floats above me, her face a smooth mask of stone, and she flicks from her fingertips a million points of color which create me in the darkness of the dreamscape canvas. In my nightmares, I am painted in guilt." She shook her head sadly. "It's like the rain, as you said. In the end, the details of accountability are lost to the deluge of angry accusation." She walked beside him for a few more steps. "And that, because you asked, is what I would say."

His mind filled with the sudden memory of his son, perhaps four years old, buried except for his face in one of those riotous pits of colored plastic balls. His throat clenched against the saturated pinpricks of accusation and guilt. He swallowed hard, watched his son sink and disappear again. "How did Prowl differ from Defiance, exactly?"

She laughed. "What?"

"You said the lions were named for their poses."

She thought for a minute, searched her memory. "You know what? I have no idea. The lions looked much the same, as I recall."

He pulled out his phone, typed in a query, scrolled through the results until he found an image of the lions side by side. She leaned in close to stare at the small screen, and she laughed again. "The only real difference seems to be in their tails."

He examined the image and agreed. "Yes, tip of the tail pointing down is apparently defiance. Tip of the tail pointing up is prowling."

She reached with her fingers to enlarge the image. "Weird how their tails look like paintbrushes at the ends. I never noticed that." Still looking into the screen, she asked quietly, "Are there things you would say?"

His breath caught for an instant, and he tucked his phone back in his pocket before speaking. "Yes."

They walked together again. "Tell me."

When his words came, they came in a painful rush, scraped like stones over the flesh of his throat. "He was nineteen years old. We were playing basketball. I was angry, but I wasn't angry with him. I was losing. I was angry." He turned to her pleadingly. "But not at him ... I wasn't angry at him."

Her voice was a whisper. "I know."

"I threw the ball at him. To him ... I don't know. I threw it hard, and as I let it go, I knew he wasn't going to catch it. I remember the look of surprise on his face as he turned into its impact."

She brushed her fingers against his wrist, let her hand fall away.

He took a deep breath. "The ball hit him in the chest and it stopped his heart. Boom. Just like that. A freak accident, they said later ... an interruption of electrical signals. He went down wide-eyed, without a word. By the time I reached him, he was unconscious, and even though I tried to resuscitate him, by the time the ambulance arrived, he was gone." He paused for a moment. "My son is dead, and all that's left is what I've done."

"And that," he finished, looking down at his hands, which he saw now were curved tightly around an invisible basketball, as though even now there might be a way to unthrow his intent, to hold it undone instead, "because you asked, is what I would say."

Jeremy let his hands drop to his sides, and they stopped walking. She turned to face him. She reached to smooth her fingers along his cheek, and then, with gentle strokes, she traced the lines of his features, running her fingertips over his forehead, his eyelids, his nose, his lips, his chin. She brushed the tautness of his neck, and then she rested the flat of her palm against his chest. They stood like that, in silence, counting out the moment to the rhythm of his heart.

After a time, Sophie took his hand in hers, and they walked together.

It was warm. There was a slight breeze. It was about to rain.

Meryl

She pours herself another drink and glances again at her phone, waiting for him to happen. Tears run down rubied legs as she swirls the glass and stares through its curved flanks at her own distortion. Married for half of her life, she examines a small smooth wristed healing from once upon a time and licks the lie of happily ever after from her lips. At the exact time upon which they agreed, she caresses the proof of his urgency, and alone, she smiles into the sound of his unseeing. All she asks is that he need an imagined version of her, a version to which she gives voice and promise. As words unfurl and time passes, she drinks her wine and tucks a rolled towel between her legs to catch the silent spillage. Nothing is what it once was, and things within give way as she pushes him to incoherency, reciting the lines of her assigned pleasure as a different sort of control is lost. When the towel is heavy with the waste of these moments, she whispers her departure, gathers the heft of her betrayal.

She trails a steadying hand along the wall as she inhales deeply; her world is stained acrid, but it still spins.

The sound of the washing machine soothes her.

Selves harm

There is a hammock.

Bodies sink within gravity's curved embrace toward the swaying center, one into the other, two versions of one. They stare together at the sky, where billowing leaden clouds, ominous and claiming, race to fill the remaining jigsaw-puzzle remnants of livid bruised above. One of them lifts a hand in dark relief against the roiling gray; she spreads her fingers wide as the other contemplates the familiar shape and span and curve of its grasp.

In silhouette, fingers dance against the sky, testing the air, gauging the ferocity of the storm to come.

They watch together as a single drop swells and falls into the seam of their bodies, dampening them both in equal tiny measure.

Fingers falter, slow their dance against the darkness, and another drop falls. Hand still held high, the girl murmurs an explanation, "I hear his voice."

Her mother hesitates before responding, and then, still staring up through her daughter's hand into the metaled sky, she asks, "Whose voice?"

"Funny thing is, I don't remember where I was. I only remember that it was crowded, like shoulder-to-shoulder crowded, except I was small, and so I was pressed to the softer flesh of thighs and stomachs. We were waiting, but we were also pushing forward; there was that sort of feeling that the mass of people was a separate bigger wanting thing, aside from the individuals ... you know that feeling?"

Another drop swells and falls, wet into the seam of them, and fingers smear in silhouette against the sky. The woman whispers, "Yes, I know that feeling."

"I was part of something hungry, some larger beast of urgent craving."

"Yes." The woman traces a single finger up the length of her daughter's upstretched arm, and with barest caress, she drags the outline of a small circle across her daughter's palm. "Yes, I know."

Their hands are revealed both against the sky now, fingers spanned as though to hold off the deluge.

Another drop falls to mark the common boundaries of their flesh.

The girl continues, "I remember feeling overwhelmed and hurried and suffocated and pressed and greedy for the object of our aching."

The mother's hand is now a fist against the dull verge of sky. "Which was?"

The girl flutters her fingers in a graceful gesture of flighted unknowing. "I seriously don't remember. I don't remember what I wanted or why we were there; I just remember the ache and the hunger and the sense of losing myself to the larger identity."

"And the voice?"

"Yes, the voice – it came from behind me, behind and above, a man's voice, strong and authoritative, and he called out, ***Make a hole!***"

"Make a hole? Isn't that a military phrase?"

"Maybe. What I remember is the absolute conviction in his voice, the certainty that he would be obeyed. I had no idea what he was talking about, but he repeated the same phrase several times, always with the same conviction that his words would be heeded, and then, as if by magic, the crowd began to part for him."

The clouds darken, coalesce, replace the entirety of the sky.

Become the sky.

Another drop falls, this one catching the angled grace of the girl's forearm and running a damp path to whorled elbowed flesh.

The girl turns her arm to examine the small path of release, and she sighs. "It was as though the world simply unzipped to let this man pass. As though the continued existence of the world depended on this man's safe passage through the beast's hunger. As though everything depended on the making of a hole."

The mother reaches again with outstretched finger to run lightly upward along her daughter's skin, this time to trace the path of the droplet in reverse, from elbow skyward to its source, and as another thick dark droplet escapes and swells against the small curve of her finger's tip, she says simply, "It's going to rain."

The girl entwines her fingers with her mother's, shadowed dampness smearing along the common boundaries of flesh, and she turns to stare into the bruised blue of her mother's eyes, her voice pleading, "I hear his voice."

The first raindrops fall.

"I know."

An old ending

He said, "Why don't we give it a try?"

She shifted in her seat, jammed the flats of her hands beneath her thighs, and leaned forward in beseechment. "I don't think this is going to be useful unless you define your terms. What do you mean by *thought*, exactly?"

"For our purposes, let *thought* mean whatever you want it to mean."

"But that makes no sense." She pulled her hands free and spread them out in front of her body, as though prepared to accept a large package. "What about simple awareness? Is awareness thought?"

"Is awareness thought to you?"

She leaned back in her chair, let her hands fall limp in her lap, and she stared at her fingers as she spoke. "It's just that I am aware, in this moment and simultaneously, of more things than you can know. I am aware of the skin that serves as casing for each of my fingers and for my being. I am aware of the pressure and the swelling and the membrane that separates within from without. I have been within and I have been without and I am both and I carry these truths in front of me, a lens through which the world exists. I am aware of frying meat and the spit of grease and a kitchen painted yellow and a hand resting against the curve of my hip and the exquisite salt of loss and the shrill surprise of the smoke alarm and the burst of blood between teeth and the tenderness of death and I am too often aware of the truth in advance of its revealing. I am aware of the paleness of my skin and its translucence. I am aware of the particular yielding to the density of my flesh. I am aware of the lighting in this room and the shadows cast not my own. I am aware of a desire to remove my wedding ring and project its shadowed containment against these walls. I exist in light because casting serves proof, and I exist in dark because I spill no darker. I am aware of the tendrilled capillaries, and I am aware of the difference made by the smallest flexion of muscles. I am aware of the bruise that has stained my left index finger dark gray, the precise shade of passage's notice untaken. I am aware of a fear of being alone and a fear of leaving alone. I am aware of the hurt of sharing and the press of humanity and the comfort to be found in turning away. I am aware of an as yet undone day in which my ones gather around the gray to mourn an old ending of me. I am aware of unwritten scratchings of pencil against paper, and I am aware of the truth that is your silent unremarking gaze. I am aware of the space I am taking in this chair, and I am aware of the space I fill behind these garments. I am aware of the choices I have made and the tightness of this waistband and the looseness of my dreams. I am aware of the birdsong outside your window and I am aware of the cold unblinking stare from the midst of wingspan. I am aware that I am here, and I am aware of the breaths I take of the air that is yours confined. I am aware of equilibrium's falter, and I am aware of the shuttering sweep of my eyelashes as I take you in and blink. I am aware of things I will not share with you and I am aware of thinking those things ... constantly ... I am aware of thinking all of these things ... simultaneously ... and I am aware of thoughts too numerous and too ephemeral to voice in the time I have on this earth, never mind the time I have in this room. I am aware of your impatience and I am aware of the depth of the hole into which I pour my thoughts." She ended on a whisper. "I am aware of more with every moment of silence into which I shovel my unrequited words."

"My *loved* ones," he corrected.

She was confused. "What?"

He explained, "You referred to your *ones* gathered to mourn. The usual phrase is *loved ones* – you left out a word."

She considered him. "I left out much, but I did not leave out words."

"So you left out love."

She stared at him for a silent moment and then gathered the invisibly flung pieces of herself into a semblance of entirety. She spoke calmly. "Alright, I'm ready now."

He fiddled with a small egg-shaped timer, and then placed it on the table between them. "The purpose of this exercise is to get a sense of the number of thoughts you have in a minute." He spoke by rote, pleased to have the path of the next few sentences laid out for him. "Many people who feel overwhelmed by the sheer numerosity of their thoughts are surprised to discover that the frequency of their thoughts actually falls within normal ranges. I've given you a pad of paper and a pencil. When I start the timer, simply make a small hash-mark on the page to denote each new thought that occurs to you. At the end of the minute, we'll total your markings and see where we are."

She pulled her feet up into the chair and rested the legal pad against her thighs. "Ready."

He tapped the top of the timer. "Go."

For a moment, she thought.

He leaned to wrap his fingers around the egg, to silence its alarm. "So what's the damage?"

"One."

Cupped light

Fern lies in bed, on the edge of not-quite sleep, and rubs her fingertips together, thumb against the others. Lightly, as if to gauge some atmospheric change that may alter the journey that stretches out ahead and into unconsciousness. There is a thickness, as though she is pulling substance from the air, a fluid that smears across the pads of her flesh, a small liquid glow that illuminates the space cupped within her hand.

When she was a child, she used to run in the falling darkness with arms outstretched and fingers darting to capture fireflies. Small pulsing glows, seeming holes in the fabric of night – she reached for them, pulled them loose from their starlit threads and made them knit for her a new blanket of comfort. The small covered jar she carried to her bedside, a lamp against the blackness, her fingers wrapped in windowed silhouette against the flicker of hope short-sustained ... within hopeless confines.

They always died.

She forgave them, but as they again and again refused to light her path, she sought ways to make the magic they held hers. She crushed their hopes within her fingertips, surprised at how easily their small glimmered bodies yielded. A small bit of smeared gleam, then, glossy smoothed against her flesh. A bit of radiance that was hers, revealing in the darkness the etchings of her fingerprints upon her skin, revealing the uniqueness of her.

A bit of light in the darkness.

Something to which she could cling.

A bit of comfort.

He says she's too needy as though she might not be aware.

Vigilance

She is who she has always been. Identity is fixed to the page with words we have agreed mean one thing and not another. With every breath, in every choice, through all the moments, she is fixed.

Yet.

Her blood stains the water ... vessel emptied.

A silver spiraled screw tightens liquid to earth.

And although flesh endures, she is somehow rearranged.

else

A fluency of birdsong

She is lately consumed with the thought of interruption. She read a poem once, whose name and author she has forgotten, about the meaning to be found in the shape one occupies in the midst of what might have been. Reaching back, she tries to recall the words, but her fingers grasp only images of a man standing in a field, his form claiming the space where other things might have happened but in that moment do not.

Other possibilities end because of the demands she makes to exist ... to occupy ... to interrupt.

Here is a world.
Here is a family.
Here is a room.

Here is a woman ... taking up space that might otherwise have allowed another version of this world, this family, this room ... to be realized. Here is a woman defined by the absence that might have been.

She goes about the days that are not hers and claims them despite herself.

There arrives a growing hollow around which she wraps her arms protectively. It is as though she is emptying out, or as though she is being filled from within by nothing ... as though the world is moving to rectify the interruption she represents in a course she was never meant to run. She wraps her arms around the shell of her and contemplates with a strange giddiness the small crack it will take to reveal that she no longer exists at all.

She walks carefully and waits for the day when she falls away from within.

In conversation with people, she leans occasionally in to confide, "The space I do not fill reveals me."

No one seems surprised.

She sits before expectant glass. It is an odd thing, the thoughtless ease with which intimacies offer themselves across the emptiness, and with a small soft click, there is a shift from here to there without moving at all. She stares at the screen, having arrived at the words of one unknown who is no more and why ... a stranger's words of absolute departure accomplished between the writing and the offer.

She skips the farewells in favor of explanation.

One moment you are standing on a beach and the next moment you are sitting across the table from your dead grandmother and the next moment you are flying through a sky of broken eggshell. When we sleep, we do not question the changes, the alternate versions of reality that appear and demand our attention before fading to give way to what comes next. We merely step forward into what arrives, unquestioningly.

Why do we question at all?

Real life splinters and shatters ... that does not mean real life has disappeared.

Only changed.

Over and over again, the world is flat, and I reach the point at which it falls away to nothing. There is a small jolt, and I am aware there is to be a rotation and gravity will release me in the turning. As the turn begins, I lower myself to the ground and reach with my fingertips for the edge of the world, exquisitely aware of two possibilities ...

Beyond the edge is a curved green world, the other half of the earth unflattened, into which, if I time the transition perfectly, I might tumble in the turning.

or

The edge of the world is a razored bladed boundary between this nothing and the next, and reaching will mean only that my blood spills with me into the void.

From sleeping to life, I am sliced by transition.

Imagine you know something is off, something is wrong. Maybe the anomaly is big and important and maybe it is not, but having noticed it, you can't stop thinking about it. Maybe it's a small lump or a sudden fluency in birdsong or a pain that won't completely ease; whatever it is, you know you should go to a doctor; you know you should figure this out.

But.

You delay truth. There's no returning to the unknowing once the words have been spoken, and you are desperate to stay in the unknowing. Within the unknowing is the possibility that the lump dissipates, the birdsong returns to foreign fluidity, the pain subsides.

You know this position is unreasonable. You know truth spoken does not change the truth that always was, and yet ... and yet. You crave the silence. Before the truth becomes a razored edge sliced against wanting grip, the silence contains softer more gentle possibilities. You want a little more time to hold the peach-fuzzed curves of perhaps.

I am consumed by change.

But maybe if I don't speak it, it isn't really happening.

Maybe if I don't acknowledge it, there is still time to caress the soft ellipse of oblivion.

The world is flat and the birds sing of endings.

I ache.

What is to come arrives.

She sits and stares at the self-taking words whose darkened lengths and heavy curves and sharpened bits of intent caress and carve the withins of her. She is at once less what she was and more. She brushes fingertips against the glow of departure and whispers, "The space I do not fill reveals me."

She is boundless sky within fragile shell.

Held.

Puzzle dust

Her hands are mine, papered over with thinner fabric. Her eyes are mine, soft bruised water shadowed by the dusty wax-bloom of ripened plums. Her heart is mine, more practiced at the slowing of the tempo.

She sighs. "I did a lot of things wrong."

"Everyone gets things wrong."

She nods slightly. "That's true, but it doesn't change anything."

"The things you got wrong are less important than you think."

"Not to me."

I don't answer, and she turns to look out the window for a moment, and then repeats herself softly, "Not to me." She gathers herself and addresses me again. "I used to think I had to make you see. I used to think everything turned on holding the moments out for you in my palms and making you see."

I reassure her, "I saw."

She shakes her head. "No. Not like I did."

I think she means to chastise me for a failure of attention or appreciation, but I see that her smile is soft, and so I ask, "What do you mean?"

She gathers up the folds of her sweater in her fingers for a moment, silent, thinking, reaching for something. When she speaks, her voice is dreamy. "Do you remember a museum I once took you to on the top of a hill overlooking the city?"

"A museum?"

"More a mansion than a museum – belonged to an early newspaper tycoon. There was a large music room, an oval room with a ceiling of molten moon." She pauses, brushes her fingers along the tabletop. "Silver but not silver, not quite. There was a hint of gold, but so slight as to be perhaps projected from below." She taps her fingers lightly against wood, her tone suddenly more present. "You know, I searched once for the word ... I thought there must be a name for the silver-gold color, but the best language had to offer me was *electrum*."

"There's not much romance to the word *electrum*, is there?"

"Exactly." She nods and allows her voice to drift from factual to dreamy again. "The ceiling was solid yet somehow malleable; there was movement to it, as though it might be tipped and thickly poured. I remember imagining that if I could only reach to scoop a handful, I could scatter moonlight in drops throughout the room."

"I like that image."

She reaches with a curved hand as though picking a ripened peach from a low-slung branch and then, with a flick of her wrist, she flings the emptiness within her grasp around the room in which we sit. She closes her eyes to better see what she has conjured. "I used to think if there was a way to make you see what I had seen, I would exist ... more fully somehow. I spent so much time trying to hold rain in my hands, trying to show you the curves of individual watered gravity; I failed to see that my grasp changed that which I tried to offer."

"I remember the mansion."

"Do you?"

"I remember it was cold. I remember windows were open and there was scaffolding outside – some sort of renovation work. I remember the trees were bare, so bare that from the windows of the bedrooms, I could see the river snaking through the city far below."

"He left in the fall," she offers as if by way of explanation.

"I remember you gave me permission to wander. I remember being surprised at the grant of freedom – surprised and pleased. I planned to explore the gardens, but I got stuck in the kitchen, transfixed by the jigsaw-puzzle pattern of the floor tiles. Green and cream, they were, fitted together perfectly."

She reaches upward again for the curve of invisibility, plucks its fruit from the air. "I remember he said he was tired of the emptiness I offered him."

"I sat down on the floor and ran my fingers along the seams of the pieces, looking for a way in."

"When he was gone, you didn't understand." She stares down into her own cupped palms, holds out the unseen offering. "You didn't understand, and I had nothing to offer but my own disbelief."

"I don't know how much time passed, and then you were there and you bent to take my hand. You needed me to see, you said, and we walked together to the music room."

Her voice is a whisper. "I thought of him as solid. I didn't know he had shaped himself to fit this world. I hadn't known the spaces into which he had poured himself until he emptied them. I never dreamed the pain that would flood to fill the void."

"I remember the ceiling glowed."

"After he was gone, the world slipped and shimmered and offered itself to me in unexpected ways ... that ceiling was thick liquid poured and held into place by expectations and the smoothing hands of willful blindness. I knew then nothing was anything except that upon which we agree. I wanted to show you what I knew."

"You had no way of knowing what he would do."

Her eyes lift to meet mine. "Wouldn't it be nice if that were true?"

"You knew?"

"No. I'm only saying looking back ... I could have known. If I had made room in my hands and in my life for the moments he wanted me to see ... I could have known."

"We can't always see what others need seen."

She smiles, "Yes, even then ... afterward ... I knew that, but it didn't stop me from trying." She shakes her head ruefully. "I don't remember the kitchen or the jigsaw-puzzle tiles. See? I was so greedy to give you moments, I replaced the moments you might have lived."

"I lived the moments in the kitchen; they were ... they are ... mine. Anyway, there was room enough after he was gone for all the moments."

I hear the pain in her next breath, even after all the years. "Yes, wasn't there? Wasn't there just?"

I move past her hurt. "We stood beneath the oval glowing ceiling, you and I. You stood, your face tipped back, your hair a rusty soft spill along the spine of you."

She looks at me through eyes that are mine. "You remember that?"

I reach for her hand, weave my fingers within hers. "I remember how you held my hand, fingers like jigsaw pieces designed to fill the emptiness between."

We sit together and stare out the window at the skeletons of trees.

She sighs. "He left in the fall."

"I know."

Kris Wehrmeister

Junco

She sits at the table alone, the morning sun making her a depthless version of herself. Profile to the glass, she is silent. Her hands rest in the opacity of her lap, and she stares down into whatever answer their invisibility offers. Her legs are crossed at the ankles. Her toes are *on pointe*, the tips pressed hard against gravity. The heel of her right foot is pressed to her left instep, the space between a slivered moon of illumination.

She is nude, the curves and softnesses of her made hard by the shimmered cut of sunlight.

A paper-doll sliced of midnight held up against a blinding eye.

Here are the details that matter when the details are carved away.

In his memory, a small dark bird, gray with a helmet of glossy black, stands against the new-fallen snow. It's not an unusual bird – a sparrow of some sort, he believes – but in the usual scheme of things, it's invisible against the backdrop of the world's busyness. Standing now stark against the erasure of all other contrast, he sees it for the first time. In the silhouette of its tiny feathered curves, there is both strength and fragility ... fear and determination ... faith and resignation. The bird is motionless as he approaches, and he is struck by a certainty that his understanding exists in two dimensions only, that there is something about the third dimension that eludes him. He leans and reaches for the tiny black-papered cutout of reality, only to be startled by evasive sudden flight. A single dark gray eye meets his as air is pressed and cast into exit.

Here, her hair is a long flat darkness behind her, a single long slice of the scissors along the boundary of her.

He sees her now.

He knows what comes next, knows that as he reaches, her dark gray eyes will flash.

Exhalations will be sculpted into departure.

Still ...

In this light ...

he might have loved her.

Banks

I call her back, because she never leaves a message. Even though the message was, "It's nothing important. Call me when you can," she never leaves a message.

"Hey. What's up?"

She responds as though I have joined a conversation already in progress. "... settled in the hospital, but they're pushing for rehab. The prognosis was good, but now there's been another. I talked with her; she was tired, the kind of tired that's a settling in for the long haul."

She sounds weird, and I have no idea who or what she is talking about. She continues, "Of course, there have been a lot of advances in the last 40 years, but you're never who you once were. It's never the same."

I hear what she's saying, but I can't seem to focus on deciphering the meaning behind the words. Instead, my mind races silently along a detour, trying to discern what's going on in her voice; she sounds as though she is surreptitiously hyperventilating through the words. There are strange pauses and gasps of intake amidst the syllables, and it occurs to me that perhaps she has just finished exercising, except my mother doesn't exercise and so she is apparently in the throes of great emotion. It is only after coming to this conclusion that I reach back for her words to examine them again.

"You're never who you once were. It's never the same."

As my listening catches up to her voice, I hear now the difficulty she is having floating her words across the shallowness of breaths. "He had a stroke. Weeks ago. Now he's had another one, and no one tells me anything."

Alright, that's helpful information. Not her husband, then, because of the lapse of time. I have three brothers; they are all younger than I am, but perhaps one of them?

She whispers, and I feel my own throat tighten in sympathy as her words scrape ragged progress to speech. "I talked to your brother, and he says he had a stroke three weeks ago. Three weeks ago. How is that possible?"

She abruptly turns her attention to someone in her world who wants something from her she is unwilling to give. I listen as her tone settles into impatient authority, pleased to hear her voice and breath calm and deepen as she refuses a request to put off payment of fees for something or other. My mother manages an apartment complex, and part of her job is collecting money from people who would rather not part with said money. My mother is in her 70s, and in this incarnation of herself, she takes shit from no one. I listen as she focuses on the other conversation, leaving me hanging; I hear the rustle of papers as she flips through her records for payment history, about which there is now growing contention. As I wait on my mother's noisy argumentative version of hold, I try to arrange the information she has shared into sense. It's like a puzzle, and I am hesitant to ask the questions that would clear up the confusion.

I consider. She said she spoke with one of my brothers. It seems unlikely the brother with whom she spoke himself had a stroke, and there is simply no version of reality I can imagine in which my brothers confide in one another, much less share personal medical information. One is still caught up in drug-hazed dreams of the stardom that will never befall; he has a band and fucks stupidity and plays at being superior to those who lie beside him in the ashes of cigarettes and hope. One is recently retired to the solitude of alcoholism after several years of pin-wheeling bladed severance from those who might claim him.

I shake off the harshness of my judgments with the certainty their assessments of me would be just as damning.

Neither of them spoke to Mom; of this I am certain.

Besides, my mother said she also spoke with a woman, as though the man in question belonged to this woman, which means none of my brothers are involved, except tangentially. It's a family member, though, and not a friend who has had the stroke; there are no meaningful friendships that tie my siblings and my mother and me together.

Alright, tangential involvement in probably far-flung family matters not exactly his business means only one brother ... the other.

The other, who has maintained intermittent malevolent connection to our father's side of the family all these years, dipping occasional fingers into the mud so that his communications with me are always messy.

"I don't think they believe you. Crazy, right? They still don't believe you."

And then my voice ... "Whatever. It was a long time ago. He's dead. You're not. Move on and do a life that is not mine."

"I took some old photos for you," he says. "During my last visit. They said I could look through the old photo albums, and so I took a bunch of photos for you. Photos of you from when you were little."

"When's the last time you went back to visit?"

"Six months ago. Christmas. I don't think they believe you. Still. Isn't that sad?"

"Jesus. Seriously? Thank you for stealing the photos for me. That surprises me ... thank you. But you've had these photos for six months? Send them to me."

"Oh, I don't have them anymore."

"Of course you don't."

"Weird, don't you think? The people who knew him best don't believe what you said about him."

"Well, I suppose that boils down to who you believe actually knew him best ... who had the most intimate knowledge. Sort of feels like I have a bit of an advantage."

"I hate when you talk like that."

"I am so past caring what you hate, I cannot even begin to tell you. So the photos ... what happened to them?"

"I'm not sure I believe you either. I'm not sure I ever believed you. You are filled with ugliness."

"Yes, we've been through this. I do not care what you believe. I will only say that you are one of the most fucked-up people I have ever known, and if you think that's down to your normal happy childhood, then I am incredibly impressed with the power of your delusions."

"Dad loved me."

"Yes, didn't he just? The photos. What happened to the photos?"

"I burned them."

"You burned them."

"Yes, on your behalf. I knew you wouldn't want them, what with all the bad memories you claim, and so I burned them. Fifty *pictures maybe ... you as a child surrounded by all the people who once loved you. It was funny watching your small-girl face wrinkle and give way in the heat."*

"So we're done here."

"You are always so ungrateful."

"Thank you."

"I don't know how you are anyone's mother. You are evil."

"And ... scene."

I wait for my mother to return to me.

When she does, she sounds tired. "I just thought you should know."

"Mom?"

"Yes?"

"You spoke to him, then?"

"Yes, didn't I say that?"

"Mom, who are we talking about? Who had a stroke?"

"Carl. Didn't I say that? I thought I said that."

Sandy's husband. My cousin Sandy is older than I am by 17 years ... when I was a small child, she was newly married with an infant son. Sandy was wonderful, filled with laughter and imagination and a magic that lit up the people around her. I remember wanting to be just like her. I remember the thick blond impossibility of Sandy's long wavy hair; I remember how it hung down her back like tangled gold, how it swayed when she danced, how it hid me softly from the world when she embraced me. My younger daughter has the same hair, and sometimes, when I run my fingers through its gleaming thickness, I am swept away at the memory of how easily love turns its back and becomes faceless. "No, Mom. You didn't say."

"Sorry. I spoke to Sandy, and she sounds exhausted. He was in rehab, but every time he makes progress, there is a new setback. She sounds tired."

"And he has known about this for weeks? He just got around to telling you?"

"Yes, well ... you know your brother ... delicious secrets and all that. It's my fault for not being in touch more." Her voice turns plaintive. "I wanted you to know, because I know you remember him. You remember us. Before everything went to shit ... you remember him. There is no one else."

I am about to say that this is not true, that there are of course other people who remember, but I realize this isn't true, not really. I was the only child old enough to remember what once was and who we all were in that once-was time. I am the one who drew the line between then and now, and so I am the one who remembers. I remember the voices and the laughter and the certainty and the magic and the smoke and the red sticky wax on the bottles of wine and I remember feeling like a part of something wonderful. I remember such a sense of inclusion; all I wanted in the world was to belong.

The strands of memory catch among my fingers as I smooth the tangles in the fading light. "I remember."

"You remember him? It feels as though there is no one left to remember what I remember."

I think back. Carl ... tall and lanky, in jeans and a t-shirt and a fringed leather jacket that smelled of cigarettes and muscles and sweat. Handsome in a soft way despite his height and angles, his hair was long and curled, the color of butterscotch. He sat cross-legged on the floor and played the guitar and sang songs about changing the world. He hung a hammock in his living room, hung it from the ceiling; I remember his long legs dangling on either side of the hammock to the floor. He liked camping and dancing and music, and he used to hold me high in the air so that I could press my hands flat to the ceiling. I remember how his lips curled in an oddly goofy smile around the fiery weight of his cigarettes and how he tapped the ashes into his palm. I remember how peaceful he seemed, how content he was with his life. I remember how he held his infant son. I remember the rolling liquid thunder of his laugh. I remember how his arms wrapped around his wife, and how she tucked into his frame. I share all of this with my mother.

She sighs in relief. "Maybe you could call and talk to Sandy."

Softly, I say, "Mom, I haven't spoken to any of them in over 35 years," and then instead of answering her unspoken question, I head off in another direction. "The girls will be heading back to school soon. It's been a long summer up here ... long and hot and dry ... unusually hot and dry." I sense my mother relaxing into the story she imagines I have to tell about my daughters, and I hesitate a moment before I continue. "The summer has been so hot, and everyone heads to the water when they can; there are a lot of lakes and rivers around us."

"I always meant to visit," she says sadly.

"The other day, there was a family who went to picnic and swim at a lake not so far from here ... a woman, a few years younger than I am, along with her two children – a teenage son and an older daughter who brought along her own daughter, who was three. They found a secluded stretch of beach away from the crowds, and they ate lunch and then waded into the water, because it was hot and because they wanted to show the little girl how fun it was to splash." I correct myself. "Actually, that's not quite right. The older woman sat on the blanket and watched her children and granddaughter play in the water."

"Were you there?"

"No, it's just how I imagine it happened."

"How what happened?"

"None of them could swim, but it didn't matter because they were only playing in the shallows. Maybe the teenage boy grabbed his niece and swung her into the water. Maybe she shrieked with delight, and so the little girl's mother let her brother venture a bit farther, a bit deeper. The water rose to his chest, but he held the girl high and the little girl laughed and splashed, and the world felt so perfect. It was such a perfect moment."

"There are no perfect moments."

"I know that, Mom. I have long known that, but even so ... this felt like a perfect moment. The sun shining down on the sparkling water, the little girl's delight, the love they all felt for one another, the family all alone on the beach ... all alone in the world, just the four of them. The older woman sat on the blanket in the sand and watched everyone she loved in the glow of this perfect moment."

"Why are you telling me this?"

"I imagine the boy slipped first. He held his niece high, her chubby little toes dragging through the water as he spun her around. The little girl shrieked with delight and relaxed into the certainty of his embrace, and then, just as he spun her out toward the middle of the lake, just as she felt his arms hold her safe, just as she trusted absolutely, the world fell away. There was an instant in which the boy could have released the little girl and saved himself, but that instant passed without recognition, and the boy slipped beneath the water with his niece still in his arms.

The girl's mother was standing just a few feet away, puzzled at first, certain her brother was playing a trick. Her heart pounded as she watched the surface churn, and she stepped to where they had been, ready to be angry and frightened and relieved and grateful all at once, ready for this moment to be over, but then she slipped beneath as well, her arms outstretched in desperation, reaching for the moment that had only just elapsed. The golden light followed her down, followed them all down.

The older woman saw it all; she watched from the sand, but it made no sense. How could they be standing there one moment and in the next, simply disappear?

She ran out into the water, clumsy, hysterical, weeping. She ran until she stood in water that rose just to her breasts, and then she saw the pale form of her small granddaughter, face-down in the water, her hair a billowed yellow cloud ... not so very far away, surely close enough to reach. The woman took another step and fell away."

"They all drowned?" my mother asks incredulously. "All of them?"

"It's an artificial lake, the newspapers said, a man-made reservoir created after the river was dammed. The unusually dry summer lowered the lake's water levels. The water was so low that the lake's shallow edges had drained away; the family had picnicked on a stretch of sand that was normally underwater."

"That doesn't explain how they drowned."

"The thing is, the river that was dammed to make the lake still runs beneath the lake, or rather, its shape still runs beneath the lake. A long deep trench with vertical sides ... the family played unknowingly at the precipice and then unknowingly stepped over the edge of a watery cliff. The water's depth went from four to forty feet in a single step."

There is an extended silence after I finish my story, a silence into which my mother eventually sighs. "Life is lived in the shallow water, but there are always trenches. Everyone encounters unimaginable depth, you included. But even so ... there are moments in which you see someone needs help ... moments in which that help can be offered without yourself coming to harm."

"Yes, I would have thought so."

There is a very long silence before she speaks again. "So you're not going to call?"

"I don't think so, no."

"But you remember."

"I remember everything."

Vanishing point

A woman's face appeared in the sidelight to the left of the door, her left cheek pressed to the rippled clarity of the glass. She remained that way, in profile, staring out to the left as though she were a window-seat passenger in the midst of a very long journey. She was on a train, he imagined as he stared at her, and she had long since lost interest in the details of the passing landscape; she was now simply tracking the never-ending approach of monotony's arrival at the horizon line. He reached for the words that captured the specificity of her attention's perspective – *the vanishing point*. Yes, she was staring at the vanishing point, waiting for something to arrive from nothing.

He hesitated but then reached to run his finger down a crease the glass had superimposed across her skin. She did not flinch, but instead continued staring off into the distance, and he let his finger rest for a moment just below the corner of her mouth. When she still did not react, he gathered his intentions, stepped back, and knocked again.

She disappeared.

He waited.

She appeared at the sidelight again, this time more alert, and she spoke without opening the door. He watched her lips move in exaggerated enunciation from behind the sidelight, whose glass now gave her the look of a woman speaking from beneath a small depth of water. "What do you want?" She pointed at the small valise he carried and the vacuum which stood upright beside him, and he watched her lips again, fascinated by the misshapen and barely submerged nature of her questions. "What's all that about?"

He slid the vacuum forward a bit on its wheels and stepped aside so that she might appreciate its impressive nature. "It's just that you've won a prize. A vacuum. You've won the contest!"

She disappeared again, and then reappeared above the water in a small chained space beside the barely opened door. "I didn't enter any contest."

He reached into his valise and consulted paperwork, running his finger down the margin until he got to her name, the last on his list. "Maren Hendrick?" He leaned back, pretending to check the numbers of her house. "Is this 1605 Blasden?"

She considered. "That's my name and that's the address, but I didn't enter any contest."

He held out the forms, as though helpless to explain the proof he held of her good fortune. "Who amongst us knows what we have really done?"

"Leave it there on the stoop, then."

He rested a hand atop the vacuum. "I'm afraid that's not how it works. The contest rules clearly state that all winners must agree to first attend a short in-home presentation about the vacuum's attributes before claiming their prize."

She shook her head. "I know how to use a vacuum. Just leave it there."

He shook his head sadly in return. "I'm sorry, but the rules are very clear. The company holding the contest has trusted me to spread the word of their product's virtues, and I wouldn't be doing my job if I just walked away." He pitched his voice a bit higher. "This is a wonderful vacuum ... a fine prize ... I'd hate to see you lose it."

Leaning her face out into the wedge-shaped space until her chin almost rested on the chain, she asked, "How do I know you're not a murderer?"

He gestured to indicate his car, which was parked roadside directly in front of her house. "That is my car. From its interior, I wrestled and unboxed this brightly colored vacuum, and then rolled it up the walkway to your front door. I have been standing at your front door with this large and expensive and bright purple appliance for perhaps ten minutes now, during which time several of your neighbors have undoubtedly taken notice of me. If I am a murderer, I have given no thought whatsoever to surreptitiousness." He reached into his valise again, this time for a business card. He riffled through what appeared to be a collection of cards until he found the one he wanted, and he handed it to her. "Perhaps this will reassure you."

The card read:

Thomas Bittern
Purveyor of stories and vacuums
Definitely not a murderer

She looked up from the card and smiled. "Well, Thomas ... what if I hadn't been worried about being murdered? What if I had been concerned you were a burglar? Or a rapist?"

"I have cards for every accusation," he assured her. When she still did not open the door, he asked, "Do you have a cell phone? One that takes photos?"

"Yes."

"Alright, so take a photo of me and the vacuum, and send it to your husband, along with my name and the information from my business card. If you end up dead, I will be captured immediately."

She paused, considering. "Are you really a purveyor of stories?"

He indicated his valise. "As I said, I have cards for every occasion."

She produced a cell-phone, with which she took his photo; she spent the next moment or two texting the pertinent accompanying information, and then she looked up. "There. My husband says hello. How did you know I was married, anyway?"

"Said so on your entry form, didn't it?"

She paused but then released the chain and stepped aside to let him pass. "Did it?"

Without responding, he rolled the vacuum into her house, and once he heard the click of the door closing behind him, he turned to her, a smile on his face. "Is there somewhere we might sit and talk for a few moments? Preferably a carpeted area."

"Yes, come this way." She walked ahead into a living-room space and indicated that he should take a seat on the couch. After positioning the vacuum beside the couch, he did just that. She herself settled in an upholstered chair across from him. "Will this do?"

"Just fine, thank you." He took a deep breath and sank back into the couch. Reaching into his valise, he took out a sheaf of papers, and began flipping through them. "Maren Hendrick ... Hendrick ... yes, here we go." He rested the papers in his lap and looked up to find her staring past him through the large window behind him. He took advantage of the moment to consider her.

He knew that she was 53, married to John Hendrick. Two sons, both grown and gone. She had worked as a schoolteacher until recently, having quit, she told her friends, in order to finally take some time for herself. Time he was fairly confident she had given over to depression ... her clothing was rumpled and too tight around the middle, as though she had recently gained weight; her hair was unbrushed and unevenly gray; her nails were untended; her eyes dull; her breasts loose beneath her clothing. Thomas realized as he looked more closely that among the finer wrinkles that lined her face, that large crease he had thought a trick of the light and glass was actually a mark of sleep, its shape the edge of a blanket or perhaps a sleeve along her cheek and down to the corner of her mouth. Her elasticity was fading, along with her interest. As she turned once again to him, he saw how very tired she was, and so he ventured, "Don't suppose I could trouble you for a cup of coffee?"

She seemed relieved to have been given direction. "It may have gone cold; I'll just heat it up in the microwave for you, if that's alright?"

"Absolutely. Thank you."

When she returned, he was pleased to see that she had poured herself a cup of coffee as well. He took the warm mug she handed him, sipped politely, and rested it on the glass-topped table between them. He brought his hands down on his thighs in decisive manner. "Let's get started, shall we?"

He had made this exact presentation twelve times before this, his final presentation, and he knew it by rote. As he extolled the virtues of the wand-extension and the suction and the various attachments, he mentally corrected himself ... the 7th of the presentations had not gone according to plan, as the winner in that case had unexpectedly interrupted him to vomit on the floor and then insist on using the wand-extension to clean up the mess. Behavior which had, in turn, forced Thomas to change things up a bit. He returned his attention to his voice, and he clicked the plastic reservoir free of the vacuum's body. "Clean-out is a breeze! Simply remove the canister when it is filled; you'll see that there is a handy FULL indicator marked on the side of the canister for easy reference. Simply remove the canister, hold it over a trash bag, and then with another click, the bottom falls away and the dirt is neatly deposited in your trash." He demonstrated the opening of the reservoir for her, holding the clean and empty canister up in the air between them.

"The bottom falls away, just like you said."

He glanced at her, wondering if she somehow had a sense of what was coming, but no ... she was simply pleased with the mechanics of the machine. He reattached the as-yet unused canister to the vacuum, speaking of the vacuum's maneuverability and the way the cord was designed to stay untangled as one moved about the room. "Is there somewhere I might plug it in so that I can demonstrate how quietly it runs?"

She directed him to an outlet, and he switched on the vacuum. It did run very quietly, quietly enough that he was able to continue talking over the hum. He vacuumed the carpeting around the couch and other furniture. "Now, you'll see a lot of commercials for vacuums where they will pick up bowling balls or marbles or some other ridiculous item no one ever has real-life occasion to vacuum." He turned off the machine and stepped to reach into his valise. "The real test of a vacuum is its ability to pick up the dirt of one's past."

She looked at him curiously. "The dirt of one's past?"

He walked around the room, releasing drifts of dark gray filth onto the cream-colored carpet from a small plastic bag as he went, ignoring her plaintive hand-wringing. "Yes, isn't that what cleaning is all about, in the end? We work to clear the evidence of the past so that we can stand cleanly in the present and welcome the future." He shook out the last of the bag of dirt at her feet and met her eyes. "Of course, the future arrives with filth of its own, which then becomes the past, which we work to scrub clean of our present so that we might once again move into the future."

Her eyes wide, she stared at the trails of darkness that ribboned around her feet. "I never thought of it that way."

Thomas re-settled himself on the couch.

Maren waited for a moment, waited for what she assumed came next, and when he continued sitting on the couch, when he in fact reached for his coffee and took a sip, she spoke hesitantly, "Aren't you going to clean up the mess?"

"What?"

She waved a hand to indicate the entirety of the room, growing nervous. "The mess. Aren't you going to clean it up?"

"We'll get to that in a bit. Let's allow the filth a chance to settle into the fibers of the path on which we walk." He slid a few brochures across the table toward her knees, as she hadn't yet retaken a seat. "I don't like to talk about money, but as you can see, the vacuum you have won is a very valuable piece of machinery. You couldn't be better equipped to deal with the lingering traces of your past."

She sat in the upholstered chair, ignored the brochures, clasped her hands tightly in her lap. "You have an odd way of phrasing things."

"Comes with being a storyteller, I suppose."

She nodded, gave the room one more glance, and then pulled her legs up tightly alongside her body in the chair. "That's right. Your card said you are a purveyor of stories."

He reached to sip at his coffee before answering. "Yes, yours is the last house, the last chapter."

Looking at him curiously, she asked, "Will it make sense, this final chapter, without the others?"

"I think so, but when I leave, I have been instructed to leave you all the chapters, so that if you are inclined to know the rest of the story, you may do so."

"Does it start with *Once upon a time*?"

"If you like. Shall I tell it to you now?"

She nodded.

He began, staring down into his hands, speaking softly. "Once upon a time, there was a boy. There was also a girl. They were young, very young, but they were old enough. They were old enough to know what it was to feel empty. Old enough to recognize emptiness in another. Old enough to know that their parents spoke out of fear more often than wisdom. Old enough to know what it was to be overcome with wanting. Old enough to knowingly choose the wrong things."

Thomas looked up. Maren was rapt. He continued.

"The girl was soon pregnant. She hid this news from her family. She hid this news from the boy as well, allowing a distance to grow between them for which she offered no explanations. The girl didn't know what she wanted, but she knew she didn't want to know what anyone else wanted, and so she kept her situation secret until the choices narrowed. She still didn't know what she wanted, but now her shape invited opinion, and so at this point she was forced to consider the voices of those who loved her and those who did not.

She felt as though she was drowning in voices. She tried to listen for her own. Perhaps, she decided, she would keep the baby. It seemed impossible to do it alone, and so she went to the boy, went to ask him if there was a way."

Maren whispered agreement, "Alone seems impossible."

"She went to the boy, but she had underestimated the hurt and the sadness her turning away had inflicted. She hadn't understood how her lack of trust in him would in turn break the trust he might have had in her. The boy released her hand and shook his head. He was certain ... he did not want this future with her.

And so she had the baby - a little girl - and she gave it up for adoption. She held the baby only once, and only for a few minutes. She ran a finger along its cheek, brushed her own cheek against a softer version of her own hair, and she felt her body ache with the promise of motherhood. She kissed the child's tiny fingers, one by one, and the baby curled its fingers around her own finger, and there was a moment ..."

Thomas paused, and Maren finished the sentence, her eyes huge. "There was a moment when she was overwhelmed. A moment in which she might have chosen wanting. Except ..."

Her voice faded away, and he continued. "Except the girl had already made so many wrong decisions based in wanting. She couldn't do this alone. She couldn't stand the thought of the alone."

"She didn't know the alone would be hers forever. She couldn't know, and so ..." Maren's voice trembled.

"And so when the nurse arrived to take the baby away, the girl held out her arms and surrendered that version of her life."

Pain ushered a single syllable across her lips. "Yes."

Thomas allowed a few moments of silence to pass, time in which he watched her come to grips with the approach of the horizon, and then he continued. "It was to be a closed adoption, and the girl was to never know who her daughter grew up to be, and so the girl walled off the pain as best she could. Time passed and eventually she went away to college, graduated, got married, had two fine sons; she left her life behind and lived a life."

"But she was always, inside, alone."

"Yes," he agreed, "She is."

Maren made an attempt now to harden her features, to stanch the flow of vulnerability. "Is that the end of the story?"

"No."

She collapsed into herself. "What more is there to tell?"

"There is the story of the boy. The boy went on with his life as well. He got married right after high school, to a lovely girl named Patricia. He and Patricia tried but were unable to have children of their own, and after the doctors determined it would never be, the boy's thoughts drifted to the daughter he had never met."

Her hand went to her mouth. "No."

"He started making inquiries, and he soon discovered that the adoption had never happened, that the child had been in several foster homes, but had never been permanently placed with a family."

Tears ran down her cheeks. "That can't be true. They told me she would be adopted. They told me no one would ever know."

"The little girl was four now, and her name was Josephine."

"Josephine? Who named her Josephine?"

"And so ... with the help of his parents and a few secretive others ... with the telling of a few small and several larger falsehoods, the boy adopted his own daughter."

"My mother's name is Josephine."

"The little girl was loved and she grew up content and happy with her life."

Maren wrung her hands, twisted her fingers in her lap. "Why did he never tell me? Do you know?" When he shook his head, she demanded, "Why are you here?"

"Many years passed, and the boy grew sick. Very sick, and there came a moment when the schedule of death became apparent. One of his nurses was a younger man named Thomas who dreamed of traveling ... dreamed of being an actor ... and the two of them became good friends in the boy's final days, comparing lives and wishes and dreams."

"He's dead?" Her face crumpled again, and tears fell. "Charles is dead?"

Thomas nodded and allowed the pretending of anonymity to fall away. "Charles spoke often of unresolved business, of bitterness large and small, of people to whom he owed explanations and others he felt owed him. Starting and ending, he said, with a woman named Maren."

"He was angry with me?"

"There was anger, yes ... anger and guilt and sadness and also love ... and gratitude ... and regret. The past is a complicated mixture, he said. He said he had found a way to reduce its elements to a handful of dust. I didn't know what he was talking about until later, of course.

When he died, Charles left behind a rather unusual will. In it, he left me thirteen identical expensive brand-new vacuums and a list of thirteen people to whom they were to be delivered. He left me money enough for the travel required, and he left me instructions." Thomas smiled at the memory. "So many instructions ... he also left scripts I was to follow and rules by which I was to abide and stories I was to tell."

She gazed around the room. "He left you his ashes."

"Yes. He left me his ashes, with directions to spread them at the feet of the thirteen people to whom the vacuums were also to be delivered."

"And you've done that?"

"Yes."

Thomas stood. He handed her the valise. "In here, you will find the names of the twelve people I visited before you, along with the stories I told each of them. The next step ... the next choice ... is yours."

He turned to pick his way across the carpet, careful not to step on the strewn paths of silken gray.

She didn't move as he made his way to the front door, but she called after him. "Aren't you going to clean this up?"

"No. My instructions were quite clear on that point. I am to leave each of you standing in the filth of the past with the ability to remedy the situation so that you might stand clean in the present, ready to face the future."

He left her there, the valise gripped tightly against her chest.

As she heard the door click closed, she dropped the valise into the chair and moved to the couch; she lay down, closed her eyes against the messiness of the past's requirements. Tucking her clasped hands beneath her left cheek, she was unaware of how the seams of her fingers pressed against and molded themselves into the softness of her flesh. She fell asleep.

She dreamt she was on a train.

Staring out the window.

In the dream, she directed her seatmate's attention to the horizon, where the nothing continually revealed the something that came next. She aimed a finger. "That's where I'm going ... the vanishing point."

And then she wept.

Because even in dreams, the future arrives with filth of its own.

Shore it up

The summer before his open-heart surgery, the future clenched within, a secret even from him, he and his wife traveled to California. They landed in San Diego, rented a car, and then traveled north along the coast; he had always best enjoyed her company in the car. There was something soothing about a plan, about distance covered, about reducing the days to segments of road to be traveled. They fell into easy agreement during these driving vacations; he did most of the driving, and she did most of the planning. In the evenings, they would sit in their latest hotel room and pore over maps and travel guides, deciding on the things they would see and the places they would stop to eat and the distances they would cover. There was reassurance in the agreement, and there was agreement on the details.

The bigger things they left behind, unpacked and strewn about the rooms of their life back home.

Bending to the expanse of map, in careful red ink she plotted their course.

During that visit to California, there was a night like all the other nights. The map was spread out on the cheap wood of the hotel-room table; he heard the paper crinkle resistance beneath her smoothing hands; he watched as red coursed over the intricacies of the map, watched as certain paths were chosen and others disappeared into the mist of all that would not be. He was filled with what he recognized as longing, filled as though all that was him was suddenly permeable to the wanting of the world. He was liquid and weighted and overwhelmed; he realized with horror that he might weep. Seeking to brace himself against emotion, he leaned heavily forward, resting his hands in the middle of the map.

There was a moment in which he imagined he might dip his fingers beneath the surface of the map and rip away the journeys that lay between all of the beginnings and the endings until there was nothing to do but be still.

"Are you alright?"

No. He was no longer certain of where his edges were; everything blurred and oozed, and he stared down at his hands as the map's choices snaked and undulated against his palms. He took a breath, aware of how little room there was for breathing now that he was liquid. He took another shallow breath and held it, as though refusing to exhale might cause the air held within to swell and press the longing back through his skin and out.

She stared at him curiously and said again, "Are you alright?"

He had never felt more alone.

Finally … finally … the world receded and settled, apart from him. Edges sharpened and became distinct. He lifted his hands from the map, and the map remained on the table, all of its possibilities intact.

He exhaled and took a deeper breath.

"Yes."

She went on, unaware of anything but agreement. "I thought we'd see the redwoods tomorrow … there are a few choices, but I thought here," and she slid crimson along the chosen journey. "It's called Muir Woods."

He nodded, still working to regulate his breath. "That sounds good."

That night, he lay awake, examining new truths like small tumbled rocks along his shores. As he shifted, he could hear them bump against one another, the *click click click* of abacus beads – a tallying and summing up of life. *Click click click* ... decisive, the sound was, and impersonal, an unseen statistician caring nothing about the end result, only the accuracy of the accounting. The clicks of loss and failure sounded the same as the clicks of gain and triumph, until he realized all was loss; he breathed deeply and slipped into the red.

On the plane ride home a few days later, he sat with the redwood tree in his lap. Not a tree, exactly – more of a sapling, the woman at the park's gift-shop had informed him. "Redwoods will grow anywhere," she had assured him. "They grow best in the cool moist coastal regions, but they'll grow anywhere."

He had run a finger over the filigreed green of the tiny tree's needles, undecided but enthralled by the grandeur of the park's enormous redwoods. "You promise me it will grow?"

She had nodded. "Redwoods, in the right conditions, can grow to be 40 feet tall in ten years."

He frowned. "The right conditions?"

She smiled. "Take it home. With a little care, it will grow to be a monster."

He liked the idea of tending to a monster. Liked the idea of leaving a monster behind. And so he bought the sapling and carried it home.

His wife was puzzled. "You don't like gardening."

He planted it in the middle of their small back yard and waited.

When the monster arrived, it took him by surprise.

There were claws and fire and teeth and a ripping from within and sirens and tears and wide eyes and sweaty hands and quavering prayers and wailing pleas and accusations of betrayal and there was pain ... so much pain ... a darker thicker deeper pain than he had known might be possible. He said nothing, because there was nothing to say, and because he knew anything he promised beyond pain would be a lie.

He was split apart.

As he slept beneath a sea of drugs, the map of him was altered. Bits of road were cut away, the new ends patched together in imitation of continuity. Lengths of thoroughfare were stripped from the flesh of their landscape and made to serve new destinations. What had always run from here to there now ran from *here* ... to ... *there*. When he woke, he could feel the difference, even beyond the pain – ripped away were all the journeys that lay between all of the beginnings and the endings of his being.

There was nothing to do but be still.

In the stillness, years passed, one and then another and another.

She died, quickly and without protest, dropping suddenly to the floor in the middle of the kitchen as though her strings had been cut.

Their children, long-grown and with lives and families of their own, learned to walk around his stillness until he became invisible to them.

His friends tended to their own wounds and time.

He missed nothing.

In the stillness, more years passed until one day, it occurred to him that he might live.

He began to take walks, collecting stones as he went. He preferred small smooth stones, stones that clicked in his hands as he tumbled them in rhythm to his steps. As his walks grew longer, his collection of stones grew. At first he piled them in small sculptures on tabletops and counters and windowsills and beside the sinks, but then he began to simply drop the stones throughout his house. There was no one to object.

He took many walks. He collected many stones. When there were so many stones strewn about the rooms of his life that walking became difficult, he began to make paths for himself. Down on his hands and knees, he shoved the stones so that routes were revealed in the emptiness. Every route he might need was circumscribed. His life shrank to what the stones allowed.

The tree stood where he had planted it ten years before.

It had not flourished as the woman at the gift-store had promised. Instead, it was spindly and bowed; even if he could get it to stand up straight, it would be only as tall as he was. He stood at the end of the rock-lined pathway to the living-room window that looked out on the back yard and the small listing tree.

Everything, he missed.

Perhaps he could shore it up with loss.

Jae

Out of the blue, her daughter looks up from her homework and says, as though she has finally arrived at the solution to a particularly troublesome problem, "Here's what I'm thinking ... If I just hit you in the same place every single day for as long as you are alive and in my life, then when they ask me to identify the body, all I'll have to do is look for the bruise."

There is no adequate response, and so she offers none.

Later, her husband stares at her as she weeps, his voice a helpless fury. "You are forever finding meanings I do not intend and piling them into a great hurt."

She looks up at him, her face soft and broken. "At least there is that, then."

He has no idea what she is talking about, and he gestures with frustrated hands for the rest of her thought.

She speaks with a sudden calmness. "You will know me by my bruises."

Kris Wehrmeister

Toaster

The world stretched away in every direction like skin upon a frame, taut and lifeless and scraped free of whatever vibrancy might once have danced within. The occasional barren tree was a gnarl-headed stake driven from above, pinning death into place, into service, into surface. Above, the sky was unrelenting in its single detail of menace, its bruised-steel gray the color of bitten frozen flesh.

Laurel pulled herself forward, tilting her head into the space beyond the steering wheel to peer through the frosted windshield at the sky, looking for contrails, finding none. She had arrived a few days earlier, dropping home through the leaden sky, and with every hour that passed, the fact of her arrival (and of her departure, years before) seemed to fade into irreality; this was all that had ever been. She craned her neck; surely there should be airplanes in the sky, some proof of departure's possibility.

"What are you looking for?"

She settled back into her seat, loosened and then tightened her cold-stiffened fingers on the wheel. She reached to stab at the controls for the car's heater. "I'd forgotten how flat it is."

Laurel's father glanced at her. "You forgot how flat the sky is?"

She held a hand in front of the dashboard vent, which was blowing nothing but cold. "What? No, the landscape. I'd forgotten how it goes forever, how the cold strips it bare."

"Nothing goes forever." He peered out the window as though trying to see what she saw, but only for a second. "It's what it is." He gestured with a thick finger. "Take a left at that barn there and then a right a few miles down the road. You'll see the signs." He sighed and repeated himself. "You'll see the signs."

Laurel turned left without signaling; there was no one outside to care where they were going. Inside the car, they both knew of the force to come and unconsciously braced against inertia's surrender. As the tires aligned themselves with the new straight flatness of asphalt, Laurel and her father adjusted their centers in parallel.

She hesitated in the silence that stretched, unsure how to talk to this man. Their exchanges in the years since she moved away had been largely filtered through her mother ... "Your father says hello. He loves you. He misses you." Laurel had been too busy with the messiness of her own life to concern herself with apathy's urgency, and so she and her father had spoken infrequently, content to pass the same words back and forth. "Tell Dad I said hello. Tell him I love him. I miss him too."

Laurel's conversations with her mother were generally superficial and perfunctory; they covered the same ground every time, neither of them sharing anything of actual import. A new recipe, a new outfit, a new neighbor, a new song on the radio ... *That's nice, Mom ... That's nice, dear.* Family by rote, each of them playing a part learned long ago and repeated dutifully for every performance.

Still, the last time she had spoken to her mother, Laurel had known something was coming. She hadn't wanted to know the details. Their lives weren't her life anymore, and she hadn't wanted to know. She knew the broad strokes – retirement, downsizing, the outrageous amount they were being asked to pay for cable, the death of a friend – but she tried to keep herself from reaching to touch the intimacies that lay beyond. That last conversation, though ... it had been a slice of bread in a malfunctioning toaster, her mother's words electric with the kinetic anticipation of destruction; every syllable threatened to be the one that sent the dialogue hurtling into the air, a flaming arc of ending. Laurel had taken note of the urgency in her mother's voice, and she had matched it, hoping to escape unsinged.

Yes ... hello ... miss ... love ... goodbye.

Me too.

Laurel had known something was coming, but when it arrived, she had been surprised it took the form of a Facebook photo. She stared at the photo for quite a while, trying to make sense of it. There was her mother, pale and almost naked, sitting in yellow sand beside unimaginably blue water, with, of all things, a duck upon her head. The duck was a brightly colored male, its jeweled feathers boisterous against the silken gray of her mother's hair. Laurel enlarged the photo to get a better look ... more garish than a Mallard ... a Wood Duck, she decided.

Why was there a Wood Duck sitting on her mother's head?

There had been other photos as well. Her father appeared in none of them. Instead, there was a stranger named Raymond. Raymond lived in Florida. Raymond owned a restaurant. Raymond was very tan. Raymond was smiling. Raymond owned a pet duck that, inexplicably, enjoyed perching on people's heads. Raymond was pouring a glass of wine. Raymond was embracing her mother.

Laurel had picked up the phone.

"Dad?"

Her father's voice had been resigned. "You saw the duck, then?"

"Dad, what's going on?"

"Well, it appears your mother has run off. Flown south. Something."

"She's not coming back?"

There had been a sound that might have been a laugh. "Seems I lack the proper plumage."

Over the weeks that followed, her mother had spoken to no one, instead communicating via Facebook, posting photos of her new life and Raymond and the duck they now shared, who, it turned out, was named Simon. Friends and family clicked **Like** and enviously congratulated Laurel's mother on her good fortune and courage.

The duck again, perched again atop her mother's head. Her mother was dressed in a long sheath of blue, her green eyes sparkling, her hair now blond.

Simon says go out to dinner.

Simon says.

Like

Laurel was at a loss.

Her father had called her, then, and after speaking of the gutters and the scent of snow's imminence and the incessant overhead sound of the birds flying south for the winter, his voice grew soft. "I need groceries."

"So go buy groceries, Dad."

"Yes, well ... she took the car."

"So rent a car, Dad. Or buy a car."

"I probably should." His voice was tired. "Laurel?"

"Yes?"

"I miss you."

"I miss you too."

"Goodbye."

Her next words fell into the lapsed connection. "I'll be there tomorrow, Dad."

And so three days ago, Laurel dropped through the frozen metal sky into what had once been hers. She rented a car and stopped for supplies, filling her cart with convenient indulgence and alcohol. For three days, Laurel and her father drank beer and ate pizza and watched old episodes of *Rockford Files* and *Columbo*. She had no plans beyond abandoning plans, and so she settled into the couch and near-silence, slightly alarmed at how the past recognized the shape of her and shifted to make a space into which she fit snugly. Three days may as well have been thirty ... time was meaningless, meted out in justice by way of badly scripted narrative and motives for murder. Neither of them spoke of her mother. Neither of them had spoken of anything, really, until the night before, when, hours after they should have gone to bed, her father muted Peter Falk's bumbling genius and turned to her. "So what's going on in your life that you can just step out and into the nothingness of mine?"

Laurel drained the last of her beer and set the bottle carefully against the others on the floor beside the couch where she sat. "My life has recently been emptied. Again." She looked at him. "Actually, that's not true. About the recently, I mean. It's been over a year – Sam moved out over a year ago, and the thing is? I don't miss him enough ... I don't miss any of them enough ..." She flailed her arm messily to encompass all the men there had ever been. "I don't miss any of them enough to want anyone else, if you know what I mean." She stood and walked to the refrigerator, grabbed two beers, turned back to her father. "I don't think I'm built for relationships." She forced a smile. "Job's going great, though. I haven't taken a vacation for years, so ... here I am." She left unspoken the fact that she could no longer remember what it was about the job that merited her enthusiasm.

Her father nodded, unmuted the television, and spoke over the smoke of Peter Falk's cigar. "I need a ride tomorrow."

For some reason, she assumed he meant he needed a ride to the hospital, although she had no reason to think he was ill. She handed him a beer, opened her own, took a deep swallow. "You sick?"

"Just hurting." He returned his attention to the television, where the music swelled around denouement.

"That's alright, then." She raised her bottle in a lazy toast. "Here's to pain."

And then this morning, they were driving. Hung-over and bleary, the both of them, each nursing a headache they did not acknowledge. She followed the signs he had promised would appear onto the freeway that appeared out of nowhere. She reached to adjust the car's heater, annoyed she could still see her breath within the car. "Dad, where are we going?"

He spoke casually, "Got a meeting to go to first. Then we'll see what's next."

"What sort of meeting?"

"Regular sort." He rubbed his hands together to warm them. "You know the drill ... My name is Jacob. I'm an alcoholic. That sort of thing."

She was confused. "You're an alcoholic?"

He glanced at her, blew into his cupped hands. "Did your mother not mention that?"

Laurel shook her head. "No. Neither of you mentioned that." She protested, "You always drank. You never seemed to have a problem."

"Yes, well ... it got worse after you moved away." He laughed, a small rueful sound. "I did wonder why you showed up with all that beer."

"I was trying to be nice. I was trying to be comforting. Why did you drink it?"

He laughed again. "I was trying to be comforted."

Laurel thought back, tried to fit pieces together she hadn't known existed. "So wait ... before I showed up, how long had it been?"

"About a year."

"Jesus, Dad."

He pointed to the right. "Take this next exit, and there's a little church on the left, holds meetings in the basement. Every Saturday at ten o'clock." She followed his directions, trying to work out how it could be Saturday, pulling into a gravel lot beside a small white church. She parked the car and turned to look at him.

"I wish you'd said something."

"Meeting starts in twenty minutes. You don't mind if I sit out here with you, right?" When he saw that she was staring at him expectantly, he raised his eyebrows. "Laurel, your mother has a duck on her head. She woke up and drove away and now she's in someone else's life with someone else's stories and someone else's plans and someone else's dreams and she has a duck on her head." He stared at her, his eyes watery. "A goddamned duck, Laurel."

Laurel couldn't help it. She giggled.

He leaned back in his seat, stared out the front windshield. "Life is ridiculous."

When she had regained her composure, she took a deep breath. "Dad, why did she leave? What happened?"

Instead of answering, he started talking about the past. "When I was a kid, maybe eleven years old, I remember a teacher giving us a math problem. Miss Shaflin, her name was. We were to imagine the earth was girdled with a string."

"Girdled?"

"It means encircled, but Miss Shaflin used the word *girdled*. I remember clearly, because all of us boys thought it was fantastic." He smiled at the memory. "Anyway, we were to imagine the world was girdled with a string that ran tightly around the equatorial line, right around the middle of the earth. To this string, we were to imagine adding five feet of length, and then we were to further imagine that the new length of string was arranged so that it was at an exactly even height above the equator and around the earth." He looked to be sure she understood, and when she nodded, he continued, "Miss Shaflin asked us what the gap between the new length of string and the earth might allow to pass through ... and she gave us choices – a knife's blade, a cat, or a car."

Laurel guessed. "A knife's blade?"

He smiled again. "That's what most of us guessed before we did the math, but the answer was that there was room for a cat to walk through the gap. More than enough room." He shrugged. "I don't remember the math of it exactly, but I remember the surprise."

"Dad, that's not an answer. Not to the question I asked, anyway."

"Yes, it is. Your mother and I have been married for thirty-four years. Imagine the marriage is the world. Imagine a string around its middle our promises to one another. Over the years, one or the other of us has, from time to time, added a bit of string to the length." He held out his hands to indicate the shortness of the extra bits of string. "So small, the additions, you don't notice the change that occurs. There's a slight loosening, yes, but you tell yourself it's just that you're comfortable. Except each of you continues to add tiny bits of length." He glanced at her, waved a hand to silence the question she was about to ask. "It doesn't matter what lies behind the additions, Laurel. Just know that the string was eventually long enough, even though it continued to encircle our marriage, that there was a space between our promises and what was true."

He sighed and glanced at his watch. "A space large enough to allow the passage of a cat."

"Or a duck."

He opened the door of the car, and he turned to her as the cold rushed in. "Exactly. Are you coming?"

"Me?"

"It's warm in there."

Laurel considered.

He got out of the car, closed his door, and walked around to the driver's side, opened her door. "Come on. This piece of shit car has no heater, and you're going to freeze." He held out his hand. "It's warm in there. They have coffee."

She took his hand, but she did not stand up. "Dad, I'm not an alcoholic."

"Never said you were. Topic for another day, maybe. I just thought you might want to listen as I made amends, as I said goodbye ... thought you might want to know where we're going."

"We?" She struggled out of the car, still holding his hand. "Where are we going?"

He met her eyes. "You're just like me. You've got nothing in that life of yours worth saving but you." He shook his head thoughtfully. "Your mother got one thing right ... in all the time I've known her, she got this one thing perfectly right."

"What's that, exactly?"

"Sometimes, to save yourself, you have to simply walk away."

"Dad, you know nothing about my life."

He said nothing, instead he just stared upward. She lifted her own gaze and was once again struck by the emptiness of the raw metaled sky. How had she come to be here if there was no arrival ... no departure ... no flight?

Her father lifted a hand and pointed. "There."

Laurel stared into nothingness until they arrived ... at first the seeming point of an arrow, growing until an enormous v-formation of soaring birds appeared, high above the earth. Her father pulled her close. "Imagine the birds are circling the earth, pulling a string behind them, girdling the world across the sky."

His voice grew hushed. "Imagine what might pass beneath."

They stood side by side, staring up into invisible directions, adjusting their centers in parallel.

She sighed, slammed the car door, and turned to him.

"There better be coffee."

Trypophobia

The conversation moves with them, but Charlotte snags a stray thread as they approach and pause, and she spools their words like cotton candy until the sugared fiber tautens and then breaks, the distance between speech and greedy curiosity lengthened beyond coherence. She runs gentle fingers over her gathered skein of syllables, teasing out meaning from the sticky tangles. She closes her eyes and replays the scene, exploring the spaces between the words and what might have filled the bits of emptiness.

....

They've just finished running, the two boys who are almost men, their bodies sculpted and inchoate all at once, their physique the unique province of the young long-distance runner. Hands on their hips, they bend slightly forward as they walk, regaining breath and equilibrium; their voices slip into the easy confidences that sometimes come with shared triumph and exhaustion. As they approach, their voices are indistinguishable from one another at first, and she catches only words that are pieces of larger nebulous thoughts.

"Suffocating ... practice ... choice ... pressure to decide ... don't know ... they want ... want ... want ... impatient ... I don't know ... I just ... they can be so much ... not like I know ... I just ... know."

Or perhaps that last was "No."

The two young men pause to stretch, close enough now that she can make out their conversation, her own invisibility ensured by her age, which is approximately double theirs.

The slightly shorter young man shrugs his shoulders. "I'm just so aware of them waiting for me to do something. You know?"

The taller young man nods. "I think it's the same for everyone."

"Even so." The shorter one runs his hand through his hair. "Even so. It's crushing."

The taller one watches as the shorter one bends to pick something up. "I know." He takes a step forward to reach for whatever it is the other is holding, and he laughs, a brief bark of not-quite humor. "Don't show that to Katie. She can't be around that stuff."

The other is confused. "This?" He holds out the item in an open palm. "It's just an empty seed pod ... what ... is she allergic to the plant?"

"No." The taller one speaks matter-of-factly, but there is something about his tone that suggests he is trying out the words, unsure of their reception. "She has a phobia of small clustered holes." He thinks for a moment. "More than a phobia, though ... it just shuts her down."

The shorter one looks up at his friend. "How can that be a thing?"

The taller one shrugs. "I just know it's real. She's been in therapy and everything ... anything with clustered little holes completely freaks her out."

The other is not unsympathetic, but he is curious, a bit disbelieving. "So what, like salt shakers?"

"Yes."

"Honeycomb? Sponges?" The shorter one thinks for a moment, searching for holes. "What about noodles? You know ... if they're all in a bowl, there's lots of little holes."

"Yeah, it doesn't even have to be an actual thing. Just a picture of little holes is enough."

The shorter young man shakes his head. "Wow. That's weird."

The taller one pauses, as though considering whether to share, and then his shoulders slump in a kind of defeat as he starts to walk away. "It would be alright, except for the pores."

His friend hurries to fall into step beside him, his voice incredulous. "Pores ... you mean like in your skin?"

The conversation fades, and she catches snippets, their voices once again indistinguishable from one another.

"Can't bear ... shower ... touch ... fall in ... leave ... parents smothering ... breathe ... crazy ... throwing up ... disgust ... done with it ... care ... kidding me ... can't do it ... secret ... promise me ... guilty ... me."
....

Charlotte looks it up when she gets home – *Trypophobia: the fear of small clustered holes.*

She spends the summer enamored of the fear, of its incredible specificity as well as its potential for complete debilitation. Flirting with the notion, she runs fingertips over the curves of a salt shaker, presses flesh hard to the pattern and licks the impress of salinity from her skin. On the countertop, she lines up small circles of dried cereal in rows and rows and rows and then stares down into the endless parallel routes to nowhere until her vision and her truths blur. She leans forward to stare into the mirror, to pinch and press and harass her skin until individual pores grow inflamed and swollen; she leans forward again to alleviate the tension, staring in fascination as holes open up to release oozing debris. In the bathtub, she lies staring up at the large octagonal shower head, its gleaming silver surface drilled with holes; she stares until there seems to be malevolence to the blind-eyed cluster. She blinks, and it is gone, leaving her oddly frustrated.

Is the fear that something will emerge?

Or that one will somehow be drawn in?

Or is it instead a fear the cluster represents a portal between realities?

Toward the end of that summer, Charlotte has a nightmare ... a dream of a million open mouths. She stands before a landscape of lips surrounding small portals of darkness, a million parallel paths to nowhere. There is a glistening of saliva over fleshed withins, and the mouths begin to speak all at once, their voices an unintelligible chaos of noise and need and meaning.

She wakes terrified and lost and unmoored.

After the dream, she puts aside the flirtation with the fear that is not hers.

In the years that pass, she marries. She has children, a boy and a girl, both at once. She does her best.

Charlotte gives herself to the giving.

The children have their own rooms, and on the wall outside their bedrooms, she hangs a bulletin board. It's enormous, this bulletin board, a huge expanse of framed soft cork. She carefully pins the milestones of their childhood to the bulletin board – a note from the tooth fairy, a tiny envelope containing a lock of hair, drawings of the family, class pictures, postcards, letters, invitations. Over time, the children add their own proofs of being – papers from school, report cards, photos of friends, a menu from a hotel restaurant, tickets to plays and sports events, their grandmother's obituary, awards for participation in band and track and the honor society and skating and gymnastics and football. There are ribbons and necklaced medals and programs and lists of things desired or hated. There are also feathers and leaves and bits of jewelry as well as ID bracelets from concerts and dances and hospital stays.

It's a mess.

Somehow, nothing ever gets taken off of the bulletin board; everything is simply pinned atop the previous history. The children grow, and the proof of their growth swells from the wall in a disheveled mass of love and meaning and remembrance. She walks by the wall every day, and every time she passes, she runs her fingers along the surfaces of things, knowing of the depth.

The children grow, and different things are pinned to the board ... college catalogs and roommate inquiries and copies of letters of recommendation and then letters of acceptance, one for each.

And then the children leave.

Charlotte continues to walk by the bulletin board, continues to run her hand along the surfaces of her life, tries to find solace in the proof of the moments leading up to this moment.

A moment in which she is utterly bereft.

With sweeping hands, she rips it all away, tears it down until the floor is littered with thumbtacks and mementos. She walks downstairs and returns with two large boxes, and then she sits cross-legged in the middle of the pile, a box on either side of her. For the next two hours, she sorts the items according to the child, none of it hers any longer. She takes comfort in the assignment and the surrender; whatever there is left of her life, she needs to go forward. When everything has been sorted and contained, she scoops the last of the thumbtacks into her palm and walks to the bathroom to toss them in the trash with the others.

When she returns, the sight of the empty bulletin board shocks her; somehow in all the flailing and ripping and sorting and boxing, she neglected to actually see what was left behind.

There is so much emptiness.

Charlotte steps closer, runs her hands along the surface; the thick cork is pitted with a million pinpoints of safekeeping pulled free. With closed eyes, she tries with trembling fingertips to read the jagged curves and raised edges of salvage, but all meaning has been lost ... each hole is just a hole like all the other holes – holes that speak all at once, an unintelligible chaos of noise and need and meaning.

Holes to the past that go nowhere.

Endlessly.

The fear that is hers.

Adoption

Hands smoothed on wooden floors ...

When I was very small, in an apartment whose rooms are vague in my memory, there was a wooden floor and a rocking chair that rolled its darker curves back and forth along the floor beneath my mother's weight as she read to me from a book of poetry.

Not children's words, but words she loved from others who had gathered their thoughts for her to give to me. Words of love and waiting and hurt and anguish and a bird staring through a window at a sleeping child. Words that were bigger than the events they described, words that gave the lesser size and heft in my imagination. I remember being so aware of how importance grew with one's attention. How the details mattered. How the details were everything.

I remember the looseness to her voice, the smile that played at the corners of her lips as she worked her mouth around the syllables and made them mine.

I remember the auburn curtain of her hair.

I remember the freckles across the bridge of her nose and along her arms.

I remember the blue of her eyes.

I remember the feel of my legs folded beneath me. I remember remembering to breathe. I remember moted dust in the sunlight's glance.

I remember the feel of the hardwood floor beneath my palms as I held my hands still beneath my thighs.

I remember the sound of the rocking chair's blades as the space that was ours was cut and pressed and sliced by wooden movement that was not progress.

I remember the golden gilted edges of the pages of her book.

I remember that she leaned into the forward tilt of the chair's rocking to whisper words of her own ...

"You are the one with me."

Book lungs

"I am currently enraptured with the idea that spiders have respiratory organs called *book lungs*."

He flips a page of his magazine, but does not look up. "Uh huh."

"I love the thought of it ... book lungs ... multi-leveled organs of folded tissues that look like closed books. Did you know this about spiders?"

"No, I did not."

"I keep imagining human lungs as actual books ... the pages over which one would draw breath ... the words across which one would exhale and then inhale to sustain life. Isn't that an amazing thought – that people exist according to the lives afforded them by the written words that live within them?" She leans into his face to get his attention, points into the writing of his magazine. "Think about it. Words live within you; words give you life; but where did the words originate?"

"Spiders?"

She ignores his sarcasm, caught up in her thoughts. "Someone had to have written the words! It's a magical thought ... a chicken and egg kind of problem."

"Assuming humans had spider lungs."

"Book lungs," she corrects him, and then she muses, "Speaking of birds ..."

"Were we?"

"I was out walking the dog the other day, and we went down to the fields by the school. You know the ones I mean?"

"Uh huh."

"As we approached, there were geese. Canadian geese, hundreds and hundreds of them, standing stock-still in the grass, staring at us, collectively gauging our progress and our intent. I was going to walk around the field and leave them be, but then ... I don't know ... there was something almost arrogant about the birds as they turned their attention back to poking around in the muddy grass ... as though they had known all along we would give them berth."

"Can you pass me the mail?"

She hands him the small stack of bills and flyers. "So I grabbed the dog's leash, and we made a sudden right-angle turn into the field and we just ran. We ran right at them. It was glorious."

He waves a piece of paper in the air. "Did you buy a single item for $19.99 from Target on the 13th and then go back into the store and buy something else for $19.99 just a few minutes later?"

"Who knows? Anyway, babe ... listen. The geese flew away, obviously, as we ran toward them, but geese aren't all that quick about getting airborne, and they were just over our heads as we ran, flapping their wings for purchase against gravity just a few feet above us."

"You didn't end up covered in goose shit?"

"No. Listen ... I have never before had such a sense of how strong geese are ... how powerful their wings are. I stood beneath the birds, and I could feel the air being pressed down against me by this flying feathered mass of beings. The pressing down of the sky changed the way I breathed; it both took and gave me breath; the air was literally forced into me against the rhythm my body would have chosen."

"Feels like maybe this is a double charge. Weird how they entered it at two different times, though."

"It was like a page had been turned. If you imagine existing between pages of a book that are just barely separated, and then the upper page is lifted away, changing the currents and buffeting the atmosphere of what lies between." She pauses for a moment, thinking. "There should be a word or phrase for that air between pages ... you know, when you riffle through a book, and there is that resultant fullness to the collected leaves, that bit of emptiness trapped within the pages. Is there a word for that accordioned space?"

"No idea. You think maybe you have the receipts in your purse?"

"Doubtful. You can check if you like, but I'm doubtful." Her voice grows dreamy. "Remind me to check later for the word's existence."

"Check later for the word's existence."

She stares at him, mildly frustrated. "Thank you. That's exactly what I meant. Anyway, I think there is no such word or phrase, and I think it should be *book lungs*."

He lays the mail aside and stares at her.

She stares back. "What do you think?"

He responds with a question. "Do you remember connect-the-dot puzzles?"

She nods. "Of course. The picture is revealed as you connect the numbered dots sequentially."

"Alright, well ... what I think is this: I think that if life was a connect-the-dot puzzle, your version of it would have millions and millions more dots to connect than my version does."

"Do you mean that as an insult? Because I am very much not taking it as an insult."

"No."

Cinching of the night

I dreamt last night that I worked with a thick silver needle to thread the stars, poking the sharpened tip through each of the golden bits of sparkle, thinking I could gather them up like jewels on a wire. Endless painstaking work as I moved across the fabric of the sky to impale the bits of illumination ... one by one ... stringing for myself the light required to find my way. When I was done, when all the stars had been run through by the sharp point of my persistence, I reached to pull the threading string tight, thinking to pull the stars from their place to my heart, to a strand I might wear around my neck.

I pulled and the darkness grew.

Confused, I pulled harder, but the darkness only intensified and then grew absolute.

At which point I realized that I had not plucked the stars from the sky ... I had instead used the stars to cinch the night shut.

The night above me was a wadded blackened expanse of fabric, its jeweled apertures now sewn closed.

I reached to touch the fabric of my nightmare, and it ran sooty and invisible along my fingertips.

My own doing, this blindness.

Silence within

He lies in bed and listens to the silence, a thick smothered silence
he recognizes from his childhood, and he knows without looking
out the window it has snowed. He reaches for his phone, checks
the weather and the time and the traffic reports; as he does so, an
emergency notice comes in with a startling *whoop whoop whoop*
– a message from the city asking everyone to stay home for the
day. He stares at the message disbelievingly as texts begin to roll
in from his co-workers, one after the other wondering if anyone
else is planning on trying to make it into the office this morning.
He texts his own decision to stay home; there's no point in going
in if no one's going to be there.

It rarely snows here, and when it does, he is always surprised at
how quickly and completely the city surrenders. No preparations
have been made to do anything but wait for the snow to go away.
He turns his phone off and slides out of bed to make his way to
the bathroom. He pauses on the way back to stare out the window
at the world transformed; the silence is extraordinary, everything
buried beneath.

Under the blankets once again, he pulls her to him, wanting her
warmth. She moans, a small sound of sleepy protest, and he curls
himself to her shape, hardening against her. He gathers her hair
in one hand as her breathing deepens and her body slackens,
gathers her hair in a ponytail and gauges its heft within the
enclosure of his grip. He's noticed recently that her hair is thinner
than it used to be. Or perhaps there is less of it. He closes his eyes

and remembers the raw silky thickness of once upon a time; he entwines the current less within his fingers, wondering if she knows ... realizing of course she knows.

No one tells you of the secrets you will keep.

He allows her hair to fall from his fingers. With his right hand, he curves beneath her lower shoulder. He fits his left hand to the hardness of her hip bone beneath softness and he pulls her to him. She is not awake, but neither is she fully asleep; by some unspoken agreement, they have decided she need not fully involve herself in his desires. She shifts to accommodate him, but that is all she does, and he thrusts against her and into her as she brings her hands up to tuck them together below her cheek. His breathing grows ragged as his movements grow urgent as his grip tightens as his pulse quickens; she is simply ... interrupted. When he is spent, she rolls slightly away and into herself, and he hears her breathing deepen once again into sleep.

What would they say if they said the things they know together?

He sits at the table. She makes him toast. He drinks his coffee and checks his email as she feeds the dog and cajoles it out into the snow to do its business.

Six inches, they decide.

He settles into his workday at home. She starts a load of laundry and does the breakfast dishes and takes a phone call, this last surprising him with its obvious normalcy. She waves a hand as she walks through the room, a gesture indicating that she will take her call upstairs so as not to disturb him, but still the sounds of her laughter carry.

He remembers a meeting he has to cancel.

Their house is on a corner, the intersection of two small ascending streets. As the morning wears on, cars begin to appear. Drivers with little or no experience with snow fall victim to the intersection's incline over and over again, spinning and sliding and panicking through the center dance floor of humiliation before giving up and turning back, opting for the longer route around the hills to the other side of the neighborhood.

After a while, she reappears, offers him more coffee. They stand at the window and watch the failure together, amused. People are ridiculous.

There is a pause and then a lone car appears, stops at the stop sign, and slowly inches forward up the hill. The man driving is too tentative, and the wheels begin to flail and spin almost immediately; the car slides backwards into the intersection. The passenger turns to the driver and gestures wildly with her hands, indicating either a course of action or her annoyance at the choices already undertaken; it's impossible to tell. In response, the driver manages to spend the next several minutes covering the same six feet of progress – a few gripping rubbered rotations and then the slide back to the curb, against which the back tires bump rudely after every failed escape attempt. The car is now resting haplessly at an awkward angle, nose pointed into the intersection but not at a possible route.

Other cars and trucks appear, and they drive past the snow-captured car as though it is invisible. Several larger vehicles manage to power up the hill; a few smaller cars try and fail and turn back; no one stops. Through the windshield, more gesturing is apparent, more assignment of tasks and blame. The woman turns to reach into the back of the car, the abruptness of her movements suggesting a gathering of belongings ... a decision to get out and walk. Before this possible plan can be put into motion, however, the driver grips the steering wheel and hits the gas hard, breaking suddenly free and then spinning the car in a graceful loop of frictionless stupidity across the stage.

There is an instant when the man and the woman behind the glass are exposed.

"Should we help them?"

"No."

Bottle of moments

He is married but not married well, because he shouldn't be married at all.

She asked him once what he wanted, and he spent a few minutes tapping on his phone to find what she thought might be a song or a piece of writing, but which turned out to be an ad campaign for a perfume. He handed her the phone, and she watched the tiny screen portray the impossible beauty of a sun-drenched love affair – tawny limbs and sculpted cheekbones and azure seas reflected in azure eyes. She glanced up at him as the music swooned to crescendo. "You want to live in the falseness of advertising?"

He reached for his phone, saddened she didn't understand. "I want that magic."

She sighed, relinquished the imagery. "Whatever magic there is in that scene is the sort of magic that exists only for a moment. It's a perfume ad, meant to be a fantasy ... meant to suggest their product bottles and delivers such moments."

He shook his head. "That's where I want to live."

"In the bottle of moments?"

"In that magic."

"Listen to me." She reached to touch his hand. "Even if you held such a moment, the reason those moments are magic is their evanescence. You do see that, right? Magic is fleeting and fleeting is the magic."

"You don't understand."

"Yes, well ... I understand how pleased I am not to be married to you."

This made him laugh.

More recently, he writes to her, among other things, of a snowflake.

"I want what ... exists in the caress of a snowflake, unique and cherished and evanescent. I want to live in the time before perfection melts into my grasp and slips invisible."

She stares at his words on the screen, wondering if he knows he is leaving, wondering if he realizes that his whole life is performed in minute iterations of departure. She thinks he does not know. She think he only sees the reaching for the next snowflake.

She writes back ...

"You cannot live a life predicated on an endless expectation of destruction."

To which he responds, "No. I want to live in the trust that the destruction never arrives. I want to live in the magic abeyance of the world and all its truths. And anyway ... you cannot decide what I am allowed to want."

She decides to try.

"You speak of your desire to live in the moments before 'perfection melts into your grasp and slips invisible.' Why do you insist that the moments after the melting are simply a failure of magic? Imagine instead that the snowflake for which you reach, with its hollows and caress, slips invisible, as you said, but see the invisible for what it is ... the hollows and caress of another small bit of uniqueness, fragile and also forgotten with the passage of time. A snowflake held tight slips into the whorls and arches of one's fingertips, fills the tiny valleys with the melted water of a snowstorm of once upon a time. A loss of shape and boundary only serves to better fit within the space of the embrace you offer."

His response is immediate: "You only understand your own life."

Which, of course, is true.

Although much of what is hers is his as well.

Held in fingertips of consanguinity.

Meted against blood.

Along the seam

"You have a few minutes to listen?"

Holding the phone, I bend to toss the dog out of my chair with my free hand. I sit. "Sure."

"Alright, but you'll listen?"

"I'll listen."

"You won't interrupt?"

"I am clear on the concept of listening. I am listening ... starting now."

There is silence on the line for several seconds, and then she asks, "Are you there?"

"Seriously? You told me to listen. Listening is quiet. Talk already."

"OK, hush. I'm thinking." There is silence for a few more seconds, and then she says, "Hello?"

"You are a crazy person. I am hanging up the phone."

"Yes, that's fine. There was something I wanted to say, but now I'm not so sure. Never mind."

Her voice as she speaks the last two words is tremulous, as though she is holding back tears, and so I say, softly, "Tell me. I'm listening."

There is again a silence, but this time I speak into it. "Tell me."

She is definitely crying. "You'll listen?"

"I promise."

I listen, first as she gathers her composure, and then as she begins to speak.

"When I was little, I spent several summers with my grandparents. I know ... a long time ago ... just listen. They lived in this big sun-filled house whose grassy back yard sloped down to a channel. Along the bottom of their property as it met the water was a railed wooden deck that overhung the channel, and to the side of the deck, there was a muddy boat launch that sloped down into the water. They had a boat, but I never saw them launch it; it just hulked huge and wooden and covered with tarps in the long graveled driveway that ran along the side of the property. I wasn't allowed to climb on it – the boat, I mean – spiders, they said." She pauses, and then continues with a note of apology in her voice, "The boat's not important. I don't know why I'm telling you about the boat." She takes a breath and continues, "Anyway, the channel ... just across its water was a wildly overgrown island of jungled green; I used to think tigers lived there." She laughs quietly to herself. "The channel froze over in the winters, and I remember feeling quite clever for visiting in the summer because I knew tigers couldn't swim."

I can't help myself. "Tigers can swim."

There is something in her voice, something I do not recognize, as she says, "Oh, I know that now."

She continues, "I used to fish off of the deck. I'd catch these little silver perch, orange-bellied sunfish, sometimes a fat-faced bluegill ... all too small to eat, and so my grandfather would help me free them from the hook and release them in the shallows. I liked to see them flip wildly back into their own world; that was my favorite part. After a time, I would grow bored with fishing, and I would swim, turning the muddy boat-ramp into a miniature beach."

"That sounds lovely."

She answers thoughtfully, "Doesn't it?" as though pleased she has managed to evoke this response, and then continues, "The first time I saw them, I thought they were a storm of some sort."

"Saw what?"

"I saw the water move, lifted and pulsed and muscled from below, perhaps 20 feet away and moving in my direction. At first, I thought there was a single large thing, submerged and swimming toward me, but then the whole broke the surface and fractured into leaping gleaming bits of taut-skinned individuality.

They were like a tornado, a surging liquid maelstrom, and I watched as they approached, overjoyed and also terrified that there was menace in the pulsing black. I stood, waist-deep in the water, my toes sinking into the mud, and I waited for what the darkness meant to bring."

The silence now is clearly hers alone, and so I do not break it.

She whispers, "They were magical – inky little rubber whiskered bullets of flesh, each less than an inch long. Thousands of them, darting and leaping and struggling for place within an entirety that itself made only slow progress through the silty water. The storm-cloud of their collective intent approached and then pulsed against me; I felt the smooth miniature curves bump against my legs. After a bit of investigatory head-butting, the turmoil turned inward and lingered beside me, as though working out the details of the detour required. I stood, transfixed by the bouncing churning combination of frenzy and water, and then I reached to thrust my hand through the middle of the school."

She sighs. "It was the most amazing thing. I felt I had run my hand straight into the substance of something ... that I could feel the individual cells of its existence. Even though I knew that what I was feeling were individual creatures, the sense was of the moving parts of a larger being, as though I had somehow been made privy to the spaces between that are generally inviolate.

As though my hand had spanned the boundaries of one world and reached into another, a world in which one might run the damp satin coolness of individual molecules and cells through one's fingers like bullet-headed raindrops."

Her breath catches. "It was the most exquisite bit of surreality I have ever known."

I wait.

Her voice picks up speed. "Over the summers, I saw them (or the next generations of them) many times. I ran my fingers through their abundance again and again, but it was never the same as that first time. I tried to recreate that moment, but they were only baby fish, swimming in a dervish to points unknown."

I wait.

Moments pass in which we only breathe.

When she speaks again, there is a pleading note to her voice. "The thing is? Lately, I've been having trouble sleeping."

"That's understandable."

"Yes, well. I've been having trouble sleeping, and I've been having these visions."

"Go on."

"I want to be sure you understand ... not dreams ... I'm not sleeping. Or if I'm sleeping, it's a different kind of sleeping than I have ever done before, because I am awake at the same time. I know that makes no sense."

"Just tell me."

"I just ... I don't want you to dismiss what I'm describing as dreams."

"Visions, then."

I hear the relief in her voice. "Yes, thank you." She takes a deep breath. "In these visions, I am standing on the deck at my grandparents' house, all those years ago. I am small, and the water is sunlit and green and undulating. I am fishing, and I catch only little fish that my grandfather unhooks for me; I throw the fish into the shallows beside the deck, freeing them but also blocking their access to the deeper water; plants and branches and a sandbar of muck hold them captive. To escape, they must flop up out of the water and cover some muddy ground before they are safe. For the most part, they don't do this, and so they list sadly in the shallows, their dorsal fins drooping, waiting for me to cast my line and catch them again. Over and over, I hook the same few hapless fish, the little red and white bobber atop the water bouncing proof of their endless fatal gullibility. I watch them as they gulp hungrily at their doom; the water is shallow enough that I can watch them opt to die.

The fish eventually turn their bellies to the sun and begin to breathe in wracking gasps, and I grow bored; I wander around the yard. I walk past the hulking boat, running my hand along its wooden hull, brushing aside a mass of dancing writhing spiders to read the painted name of the boat – Egress."

"Was that the name of your grandparents' boat? Egress?"

"I think so. I'm not sure. There is no one left to ask."

"Go on."

"I trace the letters, yellow-gold against faded blue, and then I walk down to the boat ramp. I wade in the water out to where my grandfather has strung the fish he's caught, larger fish than I ever hook. Their cold glimmered eyes stare up at me; their cold glimmered eyes stare down and away."

"At the same time?"

"Yes. The fish have been loosely sewn together, each stitch a loop ... in through each fish's gill and out through its mouth, one stitch per fish. The fish, quivering with life but unable to do more than thrash alongside one another and wait for death, stop their struggle as I approach, and they settle in a row of sideways stitches, one eye staring down into the water and the other staring up at me ... they are here and there and neither ... they are the seam.

I turn away from the stares and walk out of the water, turn right and step out onto the deck. I lie on my stomach – I can feel the warmth of the wood against my skin. I reach a hand out beyond the railing and slip my fingers beneath the water; I can feel the swell of the water even as it yields to the carve of my flesh. Back and forth, I curve my palm and scoop the water; ripples extend from my movements across the channel, growing fainter as they go. I stare out at the growing and also diminishing arc, which fades completely before it reaches the island on the other side of the channel; my impact upon the world does not extend to the realm of tigers."

I want to ask her about the tigers and how she learned that they could swim, but I want to hear the story she wants to tell more, and so I swallow my curiosity.

Her voice is dreamy. "And then there is the storm-cloud of fish, just as I described them to you before, approaching me as I lie on the deck, my hand dangling in the water.

And then ...."

I wait a moment, but when she does not continue, I urge her on. "And then?"

"And then my hand is amidst the baby fish, the same as I told you. And there is the sense of the spaces within, just like I said ... a magical feeling ... as though I can feel the individual cells of existence and more ... the molecules of the cells and the spaces between ... except ..."

"There's something different about the feeling in these visions?"

"Yes. I have this sense of being blown apart, or of flying apart, or of coming apart ... it's hard to explain ... in the memories I have, the feeling was about the fish – that they existed in two realities that I somehow experienced in a moment of duality. But now, in these visions, that feeling of the spaces between things into which I might slip my fingers ... well, it's about my fingers ... about my hand.

When the fish surround my hand in these visions, my hand is my hand but it is also the individual separate things that make my hand, and into the spaces between those smallest bits, I insert myself. I am within my hand. I am my hand. My hand is other. My hand is me."

My throat aches, and I press words past. "That sounds terrifying."

She laughs, a small laugh. "I suppose it does, but in the moment, in the moment of these visions, I want nothing more than to be separated into all those pieces. I want nothing more than to slip from the deck into the water ... into the embrace ... across the seam ... and be everything and nothing and the spaces in between."

I think for a moment that this is the end of what she has to say, but she is whispering into my mistaken understanding, something I don't catch and then, " ... for me."

"What?"

She whispers again, "I have so few secrets left ... keep this for me."

I swipe at a tear. "I will."

Moments pass in which we only breathe.

"Are you there?"

"I'm here."

"You'll be here tomorrow?"

"I will be here for all the tomorrows that will be."

She laughs, just a little. "You know what I mean – you'll come with me tomorrow?"

"Yes."

"You'll hold my hand?"

"Tight."

Character

The middle-aged son bends to the task of filling out a form and turns casually to ask his father, "Does your name have one or two L's?"

So much undone in a single letter.

The history of a man.

Invisible ink

She imagined she might find herself in him. He met her imaginings with words he gathered for others, some of which floated off the pages and offered themselves to her of their own accord. Great need met cast-aside largess. For a while, they were well matched.

Alex and Alexander.

One a lesser version in her mind.

After the while had passed, his words slipped from the pages still, but they lay meaningless on the floor, littering her path with the skeletons of their intent.

He wrote, but not to her.

Still, she imagined she might find herself.

She stayed.

Alex allowed the rush of words that revealed the things he didn't say to fix itself to the tissues of her being. She absorbed his authored silences like ink, the darkness pooling around the lesser white spaces of their conversations, the spillage highlighting the paler vagaries of his languid declarations of inchoate intent. Seeking to read truths in reverse, she studied the ghost-charactered spaces that spoke of him; alone, she traced fingers over flesh, tried to read meaning into listlessness; but the only depth was in the ink of other. She dipped wanting fingers into coagulating incoherence and blamed herself for the influidities of her own understanding. She surrendered, hoping immersion would grant her grasp, but his language only muscled through her days, a rolling liquid pulse of suffocation. Inked alienage flowed and stained the surfaces of her, pooled in the crevices, and spread itself opaque and smooth. In time, her hope settled darkly invisible against the murk-blotted pages of her days. The heavy sludge of lost nuance smeared itself into every secretive folded corner on which communication might have been undertaken, until finally, even the urgency of her own regret was submerged in the inky slough.

Years invested become a promise of their own.

They sat together in a room that was theirs. She sat at the window, her profile framed by the rectangle of glass. Alexander sat at his desk, his back to her.

She ran a finger down the pane, down the thinness that separated her from the rest of what was, stared out the window. "Do you see me?"

He said nothing.

She tried again, caressing the accumulated grime of her own reflection. "Do you see me?"

He half turned in his chair and looked at her. "I don't have time for this. I'm working."

"Yes."

He turned back to his desk.

"But do you? See me, I mean."

He didn't turn to face her again; she heard the tightness in his jaw as he responded. "Alex, I see you. You are not invisible."

"What if I am, though?"

"I'm working."

"What if I'm not here?"

"You are here."

She exhaled loudly, as though glad to have the matter settled, and examined the whorls of damp dirt in the etchings of her fingerprint where she had touched the glass. She licked the dirt from the small pad of her flesh, tasted the dull resignation of stagnancy in the bit of filth. "I think I might clean these windows."

"Go ahead."

"I read somewhere you can use lemon juice. I think that's what I'll do."

"Mmm hmmm."

She started outside, dragging a small stepladder from window to window. She sprayed each window with lemon-water, and then wiped the glass clean with paper towels. The windows were dirtier than she had thought, but she enjoyed the scented work, carefully extracting the dirt from the framed corners, rubbing gentle circles until the streaks surrendered to her caress. When she moved inside, the room filled with the aroma of lemons, and she waited for him to comment; he did not. She moved from pane to pane, scrubbing away the filmed accumulation to reveal what appeared to be nothing at all. When she was finished, the nothing sparkled with seeming absence.

She stood, spray-bottle still in hand. "Hey."

He turned. "What?"

"Look."

He stood and walked to the middle of the room, gazing through each window in turn, impressed. "It's like they're not even there."

Alex considered. "Invisibility is not all it seems."

He did not respond; instead he walked to the window that looked out over their front yard. "I can see everything now."

She looked at him, curious. "Can you?"

He smiled.

In bed that night, with hands sharp of citrus, she reached for him. Her fingers traced redolent history of her need along his flesh. In silence, she wrote the curves and lines of her farewell against his skin as he came and went.

When he woke the next morning, she was gone.

Alexander stood at the window of the room in which he worked and stared out through absence. He reached a single finger to the glass, pressed against. As he reached, the tang of lemon shifted against the warmth of his skin and floated ... offered itself to him of its own accord.

A story of invisibility and the ink with which it is written.

Insomnia

After an hour, Mabe wakes, as she has been waking every night for the last several weeks. She wakes into what might be the memory of a dream, except it never feels like a memory; it is her truth, experienced in those moments as her life. It's only after the seeing is complete that she realizes she has been there before.

It feels like a vision ...

Her body is frail and thin and tucked between cool yellow sheets she cannot remember purchasing. Her pillow is too flat and too hard, and she reaches to fluff its down; when her fingers press not feathers but the resistant stiffness of foam, she focuses her attention. This is not her bed.

The walls are a pale wet green, not a color she chose.

The room smells of something familiar, something far away. She reaches back for the memory, back to a hallway lined with metal lockers, empty except for a janitor and a puddle of mess. As she stands, he pours a thick powder into the vomit. He looks up at her, explains, "It absorbs the liquid. Some sort of chemical mixed with sawdust – solidifies the mess into chunks. Still bad, but easier to pick up."

The smell is overpowering. There is the smell of vomit, but laid over that scent is a heavily chemical mint that snakes its way down her throat like a purging finger. She brings her hand to her mouth, and he glances at her worriedly. "You gonna be OK?"

She shakes her head as her stomach heaves, and the janitor nods. "Let it out."

They stand together then, considering the messiness of truth.

He pours the chemical powder on the new smaller pile. "What are you going to do?"

She shakes her head, helpless. "I don't know."

Back in the pale wet green, she tries to get her bearings. She catalogs the stainless steel and the washable walls and the tightly tucked linens and the wall of window overlooking a parking lot and the mechanical sounds of life's mensuration and the scent of vomit camouflaged. A man enters the room, a doctor, and knowledge rushes over her in a flood of understanding.

She knows this next part. She can see the future of this next part. He will explain the finite nature of the time she has left. He will use the words "palliative" and "narcotic" and "hospice" and "acceptance." He will flip pages and consult records and he will click his pen ... once, twice, three times ... and he will use the phrase "diminishing returns," which will make her cry.

He will retreat from her tears, pausing in the doorway to shrug his shoulders and speak softly, words to excuse his powerlessness as well as hers. "What are you going to do?"

She won't have an answer.

He pauses in the doorway to shrug his shoulders and utter helpless words. "What are you going to do?"

She doesn't know.

The walls of her bedroom are a soft gray-blue.

Mabe stares until dawn arrives with proof.

Sanguinary

From my bedroom, through the open window, I listened for the sound of glass against cement. It came at regular intervals, and I imagined I could hear the change in its music as the evening passed, the notes higher as emptiness accumulated. What I needed was not the music, however, although the notes helped mark the waiting. I was listening for a very specific sound – the sound of miscalculation – for it was within the realm of errors and misjudgment that stories rested.

I never knew what was truth and what was fabrication, but I loved his words, even if I did not know the man. He was new to me, even though he was of me.

That summer, he was mine.

He was my mother's brother, dropped from the sky, come to live with us in the aftermath of endings.

Mostly, he stayed to himself, but sometimes in the evenings, he would sit on the steps in front of our house and drink from a bottle until perspective and dimensions blurred. My parents behaved during those evenings as though they had been given frightening urgent instructions to carry on as they always did. I watched them, puzzled at their exaggerated pretended version of normalcy. They were like aliens in these moments, hearty in their greetings and broad in their strokes ... caricatures of themselves.

They went to bed early those days, exhausted by the effort.

I was twelve.

I listened from my bedroom window to the melody of escape.

Clink ... clink ... clink ... the notes rising as they went.

And then there came the sound for which I had been waiting ... the sharp loud crack of the bottle's base smacking into the cement step just a millisecond earlier than my uncle had expected. A sympathetic jolt ran along my own arm; I imagined it was like taking the stairs in the dark and miscounting, unknowingly meeting floor one step earlier than anticipated, taking that next step as though the descent continued. That jarring electric bit of fear and betrayal ... that's what shook the words loose from my uncle's lips. I listened for the sound again, and when it came, I made my way downstairs and stood just inside the screen door to the porch, waiting for acknowledgment.

He didn't turn to look at me, but he swung his left arm and shoulder up and around as though to sweep me from the house to his side.

I walked to where he sat and I sat as well, the almost empty bottle between us. He breathed heavily, his whiskey-ed exhalations intimate with invitation and lament in equal measure. I knew he would soon speak, and so I sat quietly, picking at the small scabs of summer that adorned my bare legs. A thin trickle of blood ran down my calf where I opened a wound, and I swiped with a finger, sucking at the blood and then reaching to gather the next thinner rivulet.

"Sometimes when the bleeding starts, it doesn't stop." He turned his bowed head to look at me. "Sometimes, when the bleeding starts you just bleed until it's over." I nodded, sucking the blood from my finger, thinking of what I had learned in school about royalty and genes and families within which the blood ran too thinly and fluid within its boys and men. He sank his head back low between his shoulder blades and continued, "And sometimes, you have been bleeding for so long it fails to register as unusual, until your heart begins to pump the nothing that remains, and the pain ..." he shook his head, " ... the pain of empty veins is exquisite." He reached for the bottle and emptied it of its last liquid. "And so you fill your veins with fire, pump the heat where your own warmth has died ... and you hurt a little less for a little longer."

I nodded again.

He held the bottle in the air between us; we stared through its curved glass distortions at one another for a moment, and then I reached to take it from his hands. I fit my palms to its cool smoothness for a moment, and then I turned to set it down on the step beside me. When I turned back, he had leaned to me, and he whispered, "I was born a twin to death."

I dared not breathe, so badly did I want him to tell the rest of whatever that story might be.

He resettled his head low between his shoulders, stared at the steps that led down and away. I exhaled quietly as he began to talk. "I had a twin, a twin who should have been me as well. I was born and he was not, although he was delivered into this world, small and stunted and deformed. A mass of blood and flesh and hair, misconfigured and wrongly made – he was me and not me, all at once. Pieces of him came apart as he passed through the birth canal, they said. He had been dead for a while. They told me he was a monster, that I was lucky not to have been half of him ... that he was lucky not to have been born alive." He shook his head. "As though I had not been half of him and he of me, as though we had not started from the same instant and of the same material, as though we had not shared a life until he ceded it to blood poured and lost within." His voice grew angry. "Lucky not to have been born alive, they said. As though his luck ... was never to have breathed at all."

I shuddered at the thought of this bloody dead monster.

"He died so that I might live, they said." His voice cracked, cracked as though it had missed a step and broken itself against truth. "As though he sacrificed himself; as though he stepped aside and grew himself small; as though he yielded and sank away from wanting in favor of wanting for me."

I listened as I worked a fingernail under a scab on my knee. I considered how little it hurt for the blood to flow; there was the pinch of the scab's removal, but once a path had been opened, the escape itself was nothing. If not for the mess, one could bleed forever.

As if reading my mind, my uncle said, "Not all blood is red. Not all wounds are slices. Not all severings are sanguinary."

I tasted the salt of the unfamiliar word ... made a mental note to look it up later ... dreamed of being a person one day of such words.

"I have lain with death amidst its oozing putrefaction. I have lain with death and death was me. I have filled my lungs with the liquid of dismemberment."

I held my breath again, waited to match my exhalation to his words.

His voice was low. "I was born a twin to death, they said, but I think it may not be so. I think perhaps what died was not an other but a piece of me, ripped from me and formed to look like me so as to take from me."

I leaned back and stared up into the mothy shadows of the porchlight, considering this possibility, knowing he welcomed no words from me.

"I think what died within was possibility. I think what lives is what is left when all that might have been is bled away. There might have been hope. There might have been love. There might have been satisfaction. There might have been dreams. Instead, I exist, absent all these things."

He sighed. "Death makes all the difference there is."

I picked at my arm, licked at another small spillage of blood.

He said nothing more, and I sat in silence as well, shaping my lips around the unsaid syllables of the unknown word so that I would remember.

Sanguinary.

Mine.

Everything unsaid

Emily sat at the table, sipping a drink that despite its promise, tasted more of orange than blood. She listened as two women at the adjacent table talked of nothing as a metaphor for everything, as everyone always did. So familiar was the conversation that Emily could see it being assembled in front of her, a small nest built to hold these few moments in time. Offerings were woven into place ... a bit of gossip about a co-worker; worry about a child's grade in math; giddy bits of shopping triumph; an update about an older relative's health; exchanges of compliment, both real and false. Bits of nothing to build a curve to cradle the everything unsaid.

The everything unsaid ...

More and more, she found herself tangled in the syllables of silence.

On the way home, Emily stopped to buy a black marker and some tags – small sturdy manila tags with reinforced holes through which short lengths of twine were looped. Sitting at her desk, she numbered the tags in neat black-marker from 1-100, and then she walked through her house and tied tags to possessions until she ran out of tags.

The next morning, she took with her the item tagged #1 (her desk chair) and left it sitting under a speed-limit sign alongside the road. The morning after that, item #2 (her bedside lamp) she left balanced atop a mailbox. The third item was heavier (her dining-room table), but she managed to drag it into the front yard, and after a moment's thought, she went to fetch the black marker and add the word "FREE" to the small manila tag. When she returned home later in the day, the table was gone.

For the next several weeks, she carried on this way, ridding herself of one item each day. The smaller items, she left wherever she was moved to part with them; the larger items, she dragged to the middle of her front yard and added the word "FREE" to the manila tag. Not a single item was returned to her; not a single question was asked.

She bought more tags and wrote more numbers. She hung clothing from the naked limbs of a dying tree. She arranged shoes in rows along the edges of sewer grates. She left a folded pile of towels beside a garbage can. She turned her pots upside-down and hung them on fenceposts. She stood at the edge of a field and flung handfuls of silverware into the swaying grass, each utensil properly numbered and tagged.

Eventually, Emily grew impatient with this system. She dragged roomfuls of furniture and belongings into her front yard ... FREE FREE FREE FREE ... and by each day's end, her yard would be empty. She dropped bits of jewelry into the hollows of trees. She dropped handfuls of pens and pencils from a freeway overpass. She carried bags of books down to the river and spelled out messages in the sand with their rectangles.

Not a single question was asked.

She stripped the windows of curtains, stripped the walls of artwork, stripped the beds of linens.

Bare.

When all that was left was too difficult to carry, she made a path of "FREE" tags that led from the road to her front door, each tag weighted down with a small rock. She opened her door and waited. Soon, all she had to do was smile and point.

Certainly people wondered, but no one asked.

When the house was emptied of everything but the black marker, two tags, a pair of scissors, and a single photo, she slept. Curled on the hardness of the kitchen floor, her belongings arranged beside her, she slept. She dreamt of oranges.

In the morning, she carefully ripped a small hole in the corner of the photo and through this hole, she threaded a tag's twine. On the tag, Emily wrote simply, "All that is left unsaid." She tucked the photo and the scissors into her pockets and walked out into her back yard, where she gathered small sticks and grass and bits of moss. When she had collected what she required, she sat down in the dirt, and, pulling the scissors from her back pocket, she cut her hair.

The scissors were sharp, and her hair fell away in small drifts of reddish-brown atop the sticks and the grass and the moss. When there was nothing left to cut, she stopped. Carefully, then, she worked to weave the bits and pieces into something she recognized, a curve to cradle the everything she never got to say. When she was satisfied, she threaded the twine of the photo's tag beneath a tress of woven sable hair and tucked the tag and the photo into the nest.

The nest, she fitted into the angled arms of a small maple tree.

There was no one to ask of her.

She walked back into her house, now empty of everything but the black marker, a single tag, and the scissors.

On the tag she wrote "FREE" and tied the twine tightly.

And soon, as with all her offerings, it was gone.

Resonance

After the world ends, it doesn't end.

"Are we there yet?"

"No. Not yet."

The narrow road snaked up the hills beyond the small city, its twists and turns unlit and unbanked. The trees hovered close along the asphalt, twin armies having advanced on either side to the banks of a once-liquid river they could not then forge. Hidden amongst the trees, utility poles stood unarmed, dragging possible retreat up the not-quite mountainside in draped curves of connectivity.

"When will we get there?"

She wasn't sure, but she spoke reassuringly, "Soon."

She worried she would be lost, and so she turned to him and she said, "Do you know the way?"

He muscled the car around a hairpin turn as darkness advanced and folded shadows into dusk. "Yes." She nodded to herself and sat back as the certain future shrank to the beamed extent of their headlights. Uncurving light chased serpentine blacktop to their destination, and after a while, she closed her eyes, dizzied by the pursuit.

She clenched the key in her fist.

However long it took, they'd agreed. Sight unseen. No explanations.

It was simpler than she'd imagined to set their lives aside.

A hard slow turn and then the raw crunch of gravel beneath the tires announced their arrival. She opened her eyes to a cloud of moted illumination, and he said, "Let the dust settle. We're here."

She reached across the middle of the car to switch off the engine and then extinguish the headlights. A huge darkness descended, and she whispered, blindly, "I don't want to see just yet." The bittings of the key struggled to open the flesh of her palm. "Please."

"The light doesn't change what's there."

"So let the light unchange for one more night."

What little moonlight there was adjusted itself so she could discern the acquiescent nod of his profile. His voice was tired. "Tomorrow, then."

They slept in their seats. The night was warm.

He held the pencil in his fist, and the words appeared, big and round. "When I grow up, I am going to be ..."

She tried to guide his pencil. "Your daddy's a teacher. I'm a travel agent."

He looked at her pityingly and wrote, " ... god."

She woke before him and stared out the windshield at the house. It was small and unkempt, but solid looking. She knew from the property's history that it had been a rental for several years, and there was definitely a lack of pride of ownership. She sat up and considered; that's what they were bringing – pride of ownership. She reached to pull the keys from where they still rested in the car's ignition, and she fit the small house-key onto the ring.

She squared her shoulders. Woke him. This was theirs.

The key turned the lock on a hinge-splintered door.

He wandered the rooms as she ran fingertips over countertops and windowpanes. There was an odd assortment of belongings left behind; in every room, she had the impression of a succession of cars packed hurriedly over the years, the repeated realization that not everything would fit. Frustrated voices, but the same message of defeat – "We don't need it. Leave it here."

Leave it here.

In the kitchen, she counted three coffee-makers, all filthy; the one she'd brought along made four. She cleared a space on the counter and set about brewing some coffee. While she waited for the pot to fill, she opened cupboards and drawers, finding in each a jumbled collection of items deemed unworthy.

Leave it here.

She found two unchipped mugs, which she rinsed, and she poured coffee. She walked with the mugs to the living room, hesitating in the doorway, steadying herself until the twin black pools lay calm. He was on his hands and knees beside a ladder-backed wooden chair, picking at the edge of the faded green carpet. She watched as he gained purchase and then pulled a filthy stained triangle away from the room's corner. Walking to where he knelt, she said simply, "We need to get all of this furniture out of here before we can pull the carpet."

He reached to accept the coffee she offered, and then he turned to stare with her at the thrift-store collection of furniture that crowded the room. Still kneeling, he reached into his back pocket for a utility knife and held it aloft. "I'm starting with the carpet."

The things there were to say stuck in her throat, and so she said instead, as she leaned to trace the fainted outlines of a spill against the wall, "Starting is the important thing."

As if by agreement, they drank their coffee quickly and in silence, and then, as he bent to the task of cutting out sections of carpet, she walked away and to the front door, dragging the ladder-backed chair with her. Yanking open the door, she tossed the chair into the front yard, and then she turned to his back to say, "I think I might take a short walk ... just to look around."

In response she heard only the yielding of fibers beneath blade.

The yard was large and overgrown and gave way to the woods at its edges. There was a wooden picnic table planted amidst the tall grass, and the remains of a small metal swing-set as well. She walked farther and found the outlines of what had once been a large vegetable garden. She turned to look back at the house; it was an old house, and she liked the solidity of it. She liked the sensibility of its four right angles. She liked how it claimed its space in the vastness.

"I drew you a picture of our house."

"Do you want to add some doors or windows?"

"No."

It was a small house in a huge quiet. She nodded to herself.

She walked out to the road and turned to walk along it. The trees were just as close on either side as she remembered from the night before; if she stood on the very edge of the asphalt as she walked, she could touch the trunks of the closest trees with her outstretched hand. She looked up; the branches started high and arced over the roadway; a canopy of green filtered the slanted sunlight down to where she stood.

She continued to walk, counting out the utility poles as she went. The poles were planted just as close to the road as the trees, and she brushed her fingertips against their smooth grayed curves. As she touched the eleventh pole, it buzzed beneath her fingers. She stopped, surprised, and reached to press her palm to the wood. It vibrated against her skin, a tuning fork struck against the world. She stepped to put her ear to the pole; the vibrations played a single thrumming ceaseless note, but there was depth within the note, as though all of the notes of the world had been collapsed into a unity. She pressed her cheek to the music, felt it enter her flesh and sing to her of the vastness and of the space she might be asked to claim.

It was her song, and so she sang along.

"Sometimes, I am gone."

"Even if that's true, you always come back."

"Are you sure?"

"You are mine. Who else would I know to love?"

He said it again, as though it was his name, "I am Gone."

When she returned, several other chairs had joined the one she'd thrown. She walked around the broken pile and into the house. Held out her hands.

He was skeptical, and he spoke of bee-hives and the wind and transformers and resonant frequencies.

"That last one," she asked, "What is that, again?"

"Resonant frequency?"

"Yes."

He thought for a moment. "It's the tendency of a system to oscillate at a greater amplitude at some frequencies than at others. Maybe there's something about the electric frequency passing along that particular utility pole that is causing it to vibrate."

She was puzzled. "Isn't resonant frequency what causes bridges to fall?"

"Yes, because the energy gets trapped within the system, and so the waves build on one another and amplify and, in the case of a bridge, can bring down the structure that contained the original frequency."

"So resonant frequency can end one state of being?"

He frowned. "Not exactly, no."

She nodded to herself as he returned to the task of ripping out carpet. Humming, she dragged furniture out into the front yard until all that was left in the living room was a couch too heavy to drag alone, and then she dragged that out as well. The pile was a chaos of legs and arms and backs and broken supports; nothing seemed like anyone's, which made it easier. She walked around the house to topple the ancient swing-set, which fell and broke apart easily, and then she sat at the picnic table and made plans to reclaim the garden.

Later, they stood together in a corner. The floors were oak, but they were in need of repair, and some of the wood would have to be replaced. He indicated an area of messy decay. "We're going to have to pull those boards up."

She nodded.

His voice was small across the distance. "I dreamt of you, but you didn't answer."

"Where are you?"

"Do you remember what my hands do?"

"Yes."

"Tell me. I've forgotten."

They settled into the work to be done. The pile in the front yard grew. Wood was torn from the joists and then replaced. Floors were sanded and polished; the walls were patched; the kitchen cabinetry was refinished; the rooms were painted; the windows were scrubbed; the garden tilled and planted. There were endless projects, but the projects pleased them, both in the doing and in the completion. Slowly, over many weeks, they made progress on what was theirs.

She didn't mention the utility pole again after that first morning, but she walked along the road, and every morning, she stopped to embrace its gray curved wood and press its song to her cheek. She didn't care what he thought he knew; there were no bees and there was no wind and there were no transformers atop this pole. She listened to the song and she keened along; she knew the single swollen transformative note to grief.

He broke the silence. "You know what a crescendo is?"

"Yes."

"And how the noise swells and pulses until it touches everything and then it just keeps growing?"

"Yes."

"What if it doesn't stop?"

"It does."

"When?"

If she had been asked to explain, she would have spoken of the vagaries of death forced into service of the living and how there was a music to the servitude and a magic to the music. If she had been asked to explain, she would have offered up the image of her wooden embraces and the thrumming of her pulse and the metronome of her heartbeat. If he had asked, she would have told him.

But instead his inquiries were wordless, hesitant overtures in the dark from which she turned away. He curved his body to hers, a pressing question-mark of flesh, and he wept as she stared unmoved at the moonlit walls. She had picked the paint colors for the house; the bedroom was a soft-water blue.

In the mornings, his voice was matter-of-fact.

"We need a door."

The front door, having opened with the key upon their arrival, refused to refit completely back into its frame. The wood at the hinges was splintered, and the door was misaligned. She sighed, suddenly unsure why it mattered, uncertain what there was to keep in or out.

Nothing seemed like anyone's, which made it harder.

"I know."

He drove away to get a door, and she set to the task of removing the one they had.

The door was heavier and more unwieldy than she had anticipated, and once unmoored, it slipped from her grasp and fell loud and flat and into the house, settling itself like a welcome mat just beyond the threshold. She sat on the door and stared out the doorway at the contents of the house; although she knew of the effort that had gone into dragging everything outside, it looked from this vantage point as though the house had been lifted and upended and shaken empty, its contents a huge pile of unwanted.

Welcome.

She sat there staring until he returned.

That night, they lit a match and watched it burn, and when there was nothing left but embers, they closed the door behind them and slept in the soft-water blue.

They slept in the curve of question-marks.

The night was warm.

His hand was small and soft in hers, and as they walked along, he never quite matched her pace; one moment he skipped ahead the extent of her arm's tether, and the next he lingered, pressed against her thigh. He gazed up at her. "Want to know a secret?"

"Always."

"No one else can tell my story."

"Silly boy."

He giggled. "It's true! Want to know what my favorite part is?"

She pretended contemplation. "The happily-ever-after?"

His face grew serious. "No, that's not in my story."

"So what is your favorite part?"

"The ending."

Another morning arrived, and she headed out for her walk. The road was the same as it always was, and she walked along its left edge, as she always did. As she neared the utility pole she always visited, there was a buzzing sound from behind her, and she was confused for a moment; she stared at the pole, which was about twenty feet in front of her, startled at its new ability to throw its voice. As the song grew louder and throatier, she realized it wasn't a song at all, but an engine. She turned to greet its approach as the hum became a growl; a pick-up truck appeared and slowed and then fit itself into a gap between trees. The driver, a woman her age - about 50 - climbed from the truck, pulling her baseball cap from her head as she approached. She ran a hand through the gray-streaked burnish of her hair and then extended that same hand in greeting. "I'm Sadie."

She reached for the woman's hand, shook it. "I'm Gina."

Sadie smiled. "Nice to meet you." She stepped aside and swung an arm to indicate that Gina might pass. "You look like you're on your way to someplace important. Don't let me stop you. I'm just here to check the lines." She waved a vague hand to indicate the woods on either side of the road. "Trees only stand until they fall, and when they fall, they have a tendency to take things with them."

Gina pointed. "I was only going as far as the next utility pole, actually."

Sadie nodded and directed her attention upward. "I come out here every couple of weeks, just as a courtesy, checking to see the trees and lines are playing nicely together. If there's an issue, they send someone out to take care of the problem." She turned back to Gina. "Works out for everyone. Although, if you're planning on spending the winter here, there will be some outages. Guaranteed. They've got lines threaded through branches like macramé."

"Thanks for the heads-up."

Sadie eyed her curiously. "So you live around here?"

Gina nodded and waved a hand in the direction from which she had come. "Back there a ways … my husband and I."

"You're new?"

"A few months."

Sadie nodded. "Live here a bit, you'll see some things. Couple years ago, I watched one of these here utility poles swallow a car." She clapped her hands together in a sudden bark of noise. "Sideways into the pole going about 80. Car was sheared in two.

Pole went through it like a knife and then ate the half it wanted. Driver ... it was like he'd never been there at all. Like I said, the pole swallowed the ..." Her face lit up in sudden curiosity, and she abandoned her story. "Wait. Are you the couple who bought the place from Johnson? I heard something about that ... thought it was a flip, though." She waggled her hand in the air. "You know, buy it, fix it, sell it, move to the next property."

"We haven't decided. Was that accident here? On this stretch of road?"

"What? No. Other side of the hills. But about your house – god knows there's a lot that needs fixing. Johnson ain't done a damn thing with that property since he started renting it out." She paused. "They told you, right? There's some sort of law or something. They have to tell you, I think."

"Told us what?"

Sadie wrinkled her nose and pursed her lips. "If they didn't tell you, don't seem like it should come from me."

Gina decided to stop playing dumb. "About the shooting, you mean?"

Sadie's face relaxed. "You had me going there for a minute. Thought I stepped in it for sure. Yes, about the shooting. I met him once, you know."

"Him?"

"The last tenant before you bought the property. He wasn't there but a minute. Henry, he said his name was. Didn't nobody call him Hank, he said."

"What did you talk about, you and Henry?"

"Let's see ... we was standing in line at the Post Office, and I introduced myself. He said his name was Henry. He was 'bout 25, maybe. Tall. Thin. Dark hair. Hadn't shaved for a few days.

Handsome, in a messy sort of way. Messy in a lost sort of way, if you know what I mean."

Gina nodded.

"He said he had a letter to send, a letter to his parents ... I remember that, because he showed me the envelope, and it was addressed to just his mother. Not like her name or anything ... an address in Chicago and the words 'Henry's Mother' written in big letters above the address. Plus the return address, his name above that – Henry."

Gina smiled.

Sadie took the smile as encouragement. "He said the letter would explain everything. It held the key, he said. We stood in line together, and then he stepped to the counter and bought stamps enough to mail his letter. He started talking loudly as he walked away about now he had no key, and I turned to look at him, because he was talking really loudly, but I wasn't sure he was talking to me because it seemed like his voice was directed at himself, you know? But then he looked right at me, and he put his hand to his head ... you know how people do when they're just frustrated with their own stupidity ... and he said, 'Can you believe this shit?' and then he pulled a trigger in the air."

Sadie must have seen something flash across Gina's face, because she hurried to reassure her. "He didn't have a gun, you understand. Not then, anyway. I didn't think nothing of it, I mean ... nothing serious. He was just a man who sent away his only key." She explained, "He meant it literal-like, when he said the letter held the key."

Gina closed her eyes and unfolded the paper again, heard the rustle of the key as it slipped from the folds to the floor at her feet, a small metaled promise of secrets revealed ...

Dear Henry's mother,
My favorite part.
I choose this.
It's quiet here.
Come.

Sadie was still talking. "Of course, I didn't know until after the letter had arrived. Nobody did. His mother called from Chicago, called the police out here to go check on her boy. He was dead, of course. Sat in the corner and shot himself in the head." Sadie lifted her hand and pantomimed shooting herself in the temple. "For real that time." She dropped her hand. "At first they thought someone had broken in, which confused things for a bit, until they realized he'd sent his key to his mother ... he'd had to break the door down to get back in." She shook her head. "It was a mess, they said. The body, the house, everything."

When Gina didn't say anything at the conclusion of her story, Sadie returned her gaze treeward and said, "Guess as gruesome as it was, it worked out for you. Must have gotten the place for a song."

Gina walked the few steps that remained to her destination and placed her hand against the smooth gray curve of the wood. She stood for a few seconds, as though checking the forehead of a feverish child, and then she turned back to Sadie. "He was mine." She shook her head. "No." She corrected herself. "Henry ... he was ours."

She imagined Sadie watched as she walked away, but she didn't turn to look.

He was waiting for her when she returned, standing on the front steps, his expression worried. "Where have you been?"

"I'm sorry. It took longer than usual."

He sat on the top step, his head in his hands. "We have to talk. We have to get through this. I'm lost without you. Every time you walk away, I think ..."

She sat beside him and wrapped her arm around him. "You're not lost."

He sobbed. "It's just ... I don't know how to fix this, and I don't know what to do. I miss him. Everything hurts where he was, and it feels like every time I reach for you, I hurt you more." He turned to look at her. "What are we fixing? What are we doing here? Henry's not here."

She said the words before she knew them. "But I am."

His eyes filled with tears. "Every time you walk away, I worry you are gone."

Her voice was soft and fierce. "I will always come back."

She took his face in her hands.

Whispered.

"You are mine. Who else would I know to love?"

Zoetrope

In the slope of silence that followed, she rested.

She stared across the yard through the small gaps between the boards of the tall fence as he walked behind along the length and then the width of what was theirs.

Slashes of truth that hinted at a larger reality; she assembled him from vertical slices.

A zoetrope, she thought, a spinning slatted world within which movement is only an illusion.

In which repetition belies intent, and departure becomes arrival becomes departure to arrive again.

She stood in the slope of silence in the green of the yard and she spun the world and waited.

But he was gone.

16th Tile

Sensing my hesitation, he makes a show of leaning forward to rest both his yellow legal pad and his pen on the coffee table between us. Everything about this gesture irritates me; the suggestion that we are somehow off the record for the next few moments strikes me as manipulative and calculated; how many people have lurched forward into that reassurance, spilled their words into sieved promises never sealed? I stare at the empty yellow of the legal pad, knowing that anything captured there will take on a life apart from me, a life with power to change the life from which they emerged.

The pen is blue and generic, its plastic cap bitten and malformed.

This is a mistake.

He clears his throat. "What we're talking about is a bit of family history. It is sometimes helpful," he nods at my daughter, "to get a sense of perspective." He turns his attention to her and speaks gently, "I'm asking your mother to share some of what she might think are family secrets. I think it might help you to see that what you are holding inside ... the fears that haunt you ... are not so unusual ... not so scary ... that they come from somewhere that is yours."

I take a deep breath, but even so, my words come out rushed and panicky. "I'm just not sure that a list of all the nightmares that haunt the people to whom she is related is going to, in the final analysis, be that helpful. It seems to me it's a little like reassuring someone who is afraid of heights by listing all of the people you know who have fallen from buildings." I spread my hands pleadingly, my voice growing faint on the last of my exhalation. "Don't you think it might be wiser to deal with her as a separate being?"

"It's a matter of context," he says soothingly.

I take a deep breath and force a laugh over my hostility. "I don't like you very much."

He bends to pick up his legal pad and pen. "This process should be less about you and more about your daughter, don't you think?"

I try again. "Perhaps this is a conversation you and I could have privately. I don't see how including her is going ..." but then I glance over at her, and I see her curiosity and her hurt and her surprise at my defensiveness and I see that it's too late for protests. I sink back in my chair. "Fine."

He leans back in his chair as well, scribbles a few notes of blue upon yellow. He looks up at me. "Alright, so tell me a little bit about your husband's family."

"What, like just generally?"

"Feel free to share whatever you like, but what we're hoping to glean is a better understanding of the mental-health background of the two families that have made the genetic tree from which this apple has fallen."

My daughter shakes her head and speaks for the first time. "I'm not overly fond of the apple metaphor, so if that's an image you particularly enjoy, you might want to make a note of my objection."

He is startled. "Oh? Why is that?"

She sweeps stiff fingers backward from her temples through long blond hair. "Alright, well … people always say that the apple doesn't fall far from the tree, and I guess that's what you're getting at – the idea that a tree yields only one sort of fruit. The thing is, though … an apple that falls has not been chosen … an apple that falls has missed its moment … an apple that falls softens and browns and rots and is eaten by worms and bugs and birds and turned into earth again … an apple that falls is not a separate thing; it is only the possible seed of another separate thing." She brings her arms down and folds them tight against her chest. "I am not an apple and my mother is not a tree, and I have not fallen."

He is scribbling wildly, and in the quiet that follows her words, she and I stare together as he comes to the end of the point he is making and then looks up. "I can see that I will have to choose my words carefully with you."

She nods, sighs. "That would be good."

He turns back to me. "Alright, let's start with your husband's family. There's no need for names … just a general listing of history. Think of it as you would a medical history. Say, if we were examining your family for a history of cancer, or heart disease, or diabetes, or …"

She interrupts, "I would just like to say here that your comparison of mental illness to possibly fatal physical illnesses is not reassuring. At all."

He ignores her this time and holds my gaze. "So … your husband's family?"

I consider various possible responses, but in the end the truth is, "My husband's family is disgustingly normal."

She nods agreement. "It's true. If there was a literal bell-curve, they would be sitting fat and happy atop the swell of average." He writes that down. Or perhaps he draws a little curve with smiling contented stick people dancing above its crest. Either way, we have established where the fault lies.

He prompts me, "And so your family?"

I gaze down at the floor as though I might find a path – some bread crumbs of retreat my words might use as guide. "My family is filled with secrets. With pain. With hardship and struggle. With emotions and fears as deep as the waters of which they dream. I mentioned nightmares; my family lives and breathes with nightmares others relegate to sleep. But they also live and breathe with magic. With vision. My family sees what isn't objectively there. My family is filled with monsters ..." My words catch in my throat as I glance up and meet in his eyes only irritated impatience. I let the rest of my sentence trail away as I take in the unmoving of blue against yellow, " ... and the ability to see those monsters."

I turn to look at her instead, and she is rapt.

I continue for her.

To her.

"Being different is not wrong. Being special doesn't need fixing. Feeling the pain more deeply doesn't mean it isn't real, just as failing to feel it doesn't mean it doesn't exist." I swipe at my eyes. "I'm sorry. It's just that I know this journey, and I know the small house in the woods at which we have stopped. I know the single lure the man in the woods has to offer, and I know the potency of its appeal. The thing is, though ... lost is only lost if you lose sight of the choices you have made to bring you here ... to this moment and this place."

He interrupts me, "The *Hansel and Gretel* metaphor is not an apt one."

She says, "Be quiet."

He is determined to make his point. "I do not think it wise to discuss possible medications this early in the process."

She and I stare at him, and she says again, "Be quiet."

I smooth my hands along my thighs. "Lost is only lost if you abandon ownership of the journey."

She whispers, "You don't know where I've gone."

"So take my hand, and I will tell you where I stand." I extend a hand, palm up, into the space between us, and she rests her hand in mine. Closing my fingers lightly over the angles of her bones beneath skin, I speak.

"Every morning, I wake to the view through the window beside my bed. You know the window I mean ... a vista broken into sixteen panes, eight above the other in rows of four. Every morning, the truth of another day arrives carved into sixteen bits of vision." I pause for a moment, collecting my thoughts. "You know that number puzzle you used to enjoy? A small metal frame with fifteen sliding numbers within ... the goal of the game to arrange the numbers in sequence, the sixteenth space left empty so as to allow room to maneuver."

She nods, thoughtful. "I remember that game."

I lean into her memory, wanting her to understand. "The game relies on a shared understanding and acceptance that the tiles arranged in a certain sequence constitutes success. Despite this fact, it's a solitary game, a game that trusts in the value of agreement; there is no other sequence of symbols that holds meaning or value, and yet, there are hundreds of other possible arrangements, arrangements we reject because they are not *correct*."

She stares at me.

"So every morning, I wake to the window, and I rearrange the panes, sliding the fifteen moving parts within the sixteen spaces, each new arrangement a possible truth ... a possible life ... a possible reality. There is only one arrangement that is correct, that I have agreed to agree is correct, but I am able to see the other arrangements, able to imagine worlds in which each of the other arrangements is right ... is mine ... is true." I consider. "I am able to do more than imagine those other truths. Those other truths exist. I see them and they are real. But every morning I arrange the tiles of my life to fit the consensus; every morning I agree to agree. Every morning I choose."

Is he writing this down? He's writing something.

"More than that, every morning, I exist on both sides of that rectangle glass. Every morning, I arrange not only the view from within, but also the view from without. Every morning, I choose to arrange the pieces so that I am in this life I share with you and with your sister and with your father. Every morning, I look out upon the world and in upon the world and I make it so."

"Your mother doesn't mean she creates the world with her choices."

I turn on him. "I most certainly do. Every day dawns because I choose for the sun to rise as we have agreed for it to rise. Every day, I choose the world in which I will live."

She whispers, "And you're not lost?"

I squeeze her hand and repeat my earlier words, "Lost is only lost if you abandon ownership of the journey."

We sit there, she and I, holding hands.

He speaks quietly, "And so where do you think we go from here?"

She turns to him. "I only know I have no need of the 16th tile."

And so he falls away.

Against herself

Beatrice read the other day that Adirondack chairs are clichéd, embarrassingly clunky symbols of avarice for the serenity of plenty. "They're perfect for gazing across green expanses of lawn at the distant wash of sea against sand," the article stated, "but in your small untended back yard, these chairs speak only of what you cannot see in your own life." She hates when words meant to be generally judgmental prick her individually, and she shudders to think what the writer would think of her own Adirondack chairs – stackable blue plastic, arranged within the shady cool of her small untended yard. She meant for the chairs to be wooden, heavy and cumbersome and settled (if she were to be honest) on the expansive lawn of a waterfront home, but she could never justify the expense or the dream, and so, in a moment of angry wanting and surrender twined, she purchased relinquishment in a nesting stack of four.

The now faded chairs are hers alone, arranged in a circle of impotent intimacy.

"Why would we sit in the back yard?" her children asked, their eyebrows high as, over time, they listed their objections, "There are bees and mosquitoes and ants and birds and splinters and the sun is bright and it's too cold and it's too hot and it's raining and I'm sweaty and the chairs are sticky with sap that's fallen from the trees and everything's dirty and I have better things to do and what would we talk about in the back yard we can't talk about in the house, anyway?"

Her husband was even less inclined to humor her. "I hate everything about those chairs. I hate the blue. I hate the plastic. I hate the unyielding feel of them when I sit, and I hate how they make me look up and across the world as though I am being taught a lesson to which I must pay particular attention. I have better things to do than sit beneath the sky, and anyway, what would we talk about in the back yard we can't talk about in the house?"

Beatrice pours a glass of wine and walks out into the yard, carrying the bottle with her. Settling herself into the support of not quite what she wanted, she stares out across the tangle of what is hers. She takes a sip, and then another; drinking alone is a warning sign of alcoholism and depression, but she's tired of heeding signs that merely warn against herself.

This part of life, the part after the decisions but before the denouement – the endurance; this part is difficult.

Not that she's alone.

She refills her glass and stares up through the trees at the blue shards of stained-glass sky, drinks a toast to togetherness.

. . . .

"What are you doing?"

He looked up from clipping his toenails, "Clipping my toenails."

"Yeah, I see that. Why are you hunched there on the floor beside the bed to do it?"

A guilty look flashed across his face as a toenail clipping shot across the room and was lost in the carpet. "Sorry. I should be doing this in the bathroom. It seemed urgent."

She stared at him, the staccato report of the clippers a drumbeat to her disbelief and irritation. "Sometimes, I don't understand you at all." The two of them existed together in the stretch of not-quite silence that followed, her eyes tracking the tiny flights of curved detritus cast and lost. When he was done, he made a show of collecting the clippings into his palm, but when he stood, his hands were clearly empty.

His voice was embarrassed. "We need to change the sheets."

She was confused. "What?"

He pulled the blankets of their bed down and shrugged helplessly. "I guess my toenails were sharp." He gestured at the sheet, and they stared together at the ravaging; it looked as though some clawed animal had been trapped beneath the sheet and ripped itself free; the sheet was ruined, shredded beyond repair and beyond credulity.

She turned to meet his eyes. "You did this?"

"Apparently."

It was as close to an intimacy as they had shared in a very long time.

They worked together to erase the evidence of this mutual failing. She helped him change the sheets, helped him make the bed. She vacuumed the carpet and then pulled the ruined sheet to her chest, wadding it into a ball as she walked to throw it away, trying to remember the last time they'd had sex. Trying to remember the last time she had reached for him, the last time either one of them had crossed the middle boundary of their sleep. Trying to remember the last time she had touched his naked body. Trying to remember the last time she had noticed or cared about his physical appearance.

Weeks ... months ... a very long time.

Long enough to carve proof of neglect.

. . . .

Beatrice drains her glass and pours again, staring out across her small untended back yard at all she cannot see in her own life.

This part is difficult.

Haiku for Anerin

Anerin held a hand in front of her face, carving a defensive silhouette against the glare of molten silence. No longer certain of anything, she said his name as though it might have changed. "Matthew?" The man driving the car said nothing, which he did a lot lately. It was, she thought, as though all of her words had somehow been rendered metaphorical. No responses were required.

She closed her eyes and brought her sun-warmed hand to her face, tracing in the golden darkness the curves and sharpnesses of her features. Settling fingers lightly along her neck, she willed dissociation; is this how she would feel were he to reach? She said his name again, unsure this time if she spoke the syllables aloud. "Matthew."

In the silence that followed, she sketched the contours of their marriage.

Her fingertips met nothing; this is how it would feel were she to reach.

When, after a time, she opened her eyes again, the backdrop of their journey had changed. The lush green of forested hills had given way to ravaged devastation. The vertical lines of naked limbless death stood stark against the ashen swells of hillside. It was beautiful, this lifelessness ... this ruination. Old devastation, the burning, but the wind-swept proof of dying filled the air and forced its way on every inhalation.

"Matthew," she thought but did not say.

What was it the counselor had said ... that she needed to learn to take comfort in the things she could control. "Count the moments and release the years," he had suggested, leaving unspoken the truth that the years had already wrestled themselves free of her grasp. She turned to her husband again, willing him to speak, wondering if he had been given similar advice about the value of the smaller increment.

"Learn to count syllables instead of conversations," she imagined. Fingers to her pulse, she counted the syllables of departure against proof of life. Counted the moments as the years slipped free.

I'm not sure I ever loved you.

eight

I want more than this.

five

You're not who I thought I would need.

eight

I'm sorry.

three

She repeated the words like a song, played them in her mind until they lost all meaning and until she couldn't remember who had said what, which didn't matter, because in their end, they were one.

I'm not sure I ever loved you
I want more than this
You're not who I thought I would need
I'm sorry

"Matthew?"

The devastation seemed to go on forever, stretching to the horizon in all directions, but they kept traveling, and there came a mile in which the outer limits were revealed. After the devastation, there was a small secluded lake. He turned and then turned again and then stopped the car abruptly, and they sat for a moment as the graveled dust of their arrival billowed over and resettled itself. When they got out of the car, each door slammed punctuation into the unsaid.

They walked the small grassy slope down to the lake.

Matthew

Stripped off their clothes without exchanging a word.

Matthew

Waded into the water.

Matthew

Stood side by side ... still.

Like the trees, she thought, lifeless.

Naked limbless ruination.

Arms at her sides, her fingertips met resistance; this is how it would feel to reach.

So she did not.

Matthew

did not.

On the journey back the way they'd come, she noticed for the first time there were signs along the roadside inviting travelers to **Fire interpretive kiosks**.

As she stared, Matthew asked, "Do you want to stop?"

She shook her head. What was there to learn?

Fire consumed.

"Matthew?"

He glanced at her.

She asked, "Where are we going?"

He said, "Home."

Anerin leaned her head against the glass and counted the syllables and moments left to her as the day wore on …

her face in soft light
pressed against the hard landscape
of better judgment

Greedy absorbency

In the morning, she sat disheveled and unshelved in the faded blue upholstery of his couch, her legs pulled up against her body, the soft cotton of his borrowed T-shirt pulled over her nudity and her knees. She tucked the excess material beneath her ass, pinned the hem down with her heels. She smoothed her hands over the tautness of the cotton, enjoying the sensation of substance giving way to absence where fabric spanned the spaces unfilled. Wrapping her arms tightly around her covered legs, she lowered her face sideways to her body and rested against herself; the collar now stretched wide enough that her cheek met bare rounded warmth of knees.

She adjusted her view, resting her forehead to stare down through the collar into the shadows of her flesh. Pulling herself together more tightly, willing containment, she was entranced by the dark vertexed seams of her body. She loosened and then gathered herself once again and watched as darkness shifted and peeled away and then resettled along the lines of origin.

Behind her, she heard purposeful footsteps below the more insistent noises of cups and spoons. She lifted her head to inhale the wafted scent of coffee, settled her chin into the valley between her knees. The shirt's collar pressed against her lips, and she opened her mouth slightly to allow the fabric to continue its course undetoured. She resealed the line of her lips over the thickness of the t-shirt's collar, relishing the absorption ... the wicking away of moisture.

She released her hold, wet her lips, pulled a new dry section of the shirt's collar to her mouth.

And again.

"Coffee?"

She lifted her face to him; her lower lip for an instant distended by the ragged dragged departure of wanting. She lifted her hands as well. "Thank you."

They sat in a silence he found comfortable.

She sipped her coffee and unbound herself, extending one leg and then another from beneath his shirt. The shirt was misshapen and pulled beyond its capacity to revert; with her free hand, she arranged the fabric around herself, smoothing wrinkles and pressing down the curves of dampness. She backed herself into a corner of the couch and turned sideways, settled the lengths of her legs, rested her feet in his lap. She took another sip of coffee and then spoke over the foreshortened circle of the cup's rim. "Have you ever finished a book and then pressed the greedy absorbency of the closed pages against the dampness of your lips?"

"What?"

There was no going back now. "Have you ever been so in love with a story, you didn't want it to end? Have you ever read the last words and turned the last page and been filled with a wanting for more? The kind of wanting that's a physical aching hunger?"

He said nothing, and so she said more.

"I want to know." She ran a tracing finger along collared moisture. "Have you ever pressed dry collected pages against the open-mouthed kiss of your lips? Have you ever felt the greedy absorbency of a story wanting back from you? Of a story's taking?"

He rested a hand on her shin. "Truth? It may hurt."

She was surprised at his words. "Tell me."

"I rarely finish a book. I get to the part I am satisfied with and then stop reading."

She stared at him. "That can't be right."

He shrugged. "Even so."

She was incredulous. She pulled her feet from his lap, felt the slide of his fingers along her skin as she withdrew. She said the words again. "That can't be right."

He shrugged again and sipped his coffee, and they sat together in a silence he found comfortable. As the silence passed, she asked, "How did you know it would hurt?"

"Excuse me?"

"When you offered me the truth, you said it might hurt. How did you know?"

"What?" He glanced at her. "You are always hurt when I am not you."

She spoke haltingly, unable to find better words. "That can't be right."

"Even so."

Texts

Over the years, Julia has come to expect the occasional late-night text.

October 18, 2003

3:12 am – I need your help. Please call me at a more appropriate time to discuss things nonsensical.

3:23 am – Apologies for incoming warnings.

3:24 am – Between us.

Julia sometimes responds to the texts, sometimes calls when he asks her to call, but she has learned he isn't looking for a response; any words from her end the one-sided conversations. The last time they spoke on the phone was in 1999, right after her first daughter was born, and he said simply, "Do it better than they did. This is your brother."

Which she knew.

This coming summer, Julia's older daughter will turn 16.

May 12, 2005

3:11 am – Obligation? Obviously not, but I do need your help.

3:31 am – The madhouse mirrors are the only ones that lie.

3:32 am – A childhood of mirrors and untruths. How do we do it?

3:40 am – I think I just need to sleep. Is there a life so quiet as to allow sleep?

3:41 am – I need you.

She calls him that time, leaves several messages, which he ignores.

July 27, 2006

1:17 am – You already helped me.

1:31 am – Help is for the wicked.

1:57 am – Typo ... from

He only reaches to prove that she can't touch him. When she reaches, it is only to assure him he is untouchable. Or perhaps she reaches to prove to herself that the distance between there and here is too great to be spanned by need.

September 2, 2008

2:20 am – Is it alcoholism if you need the poison to kill the poison?

The only thing she can think to say, he already knows.

4:39 am – Toxicity compels.

That.

January 13, 2010

4:02 am – I knew even as I spoke I was dodging the repercussions. I protected myself, so to speak. The overdue fines have accumulated.

4:03 am – What is the worth of a privilege if it costs you everything?

4:07 am – Don't worry. I don't need you to be more than you are. Being more than I am has always been the issue.

She isn't always certain the messages are intended for her.

March 13, 2012

2:46 am – Excess emotion fraught with passive-aggression.

2:47 am – The too much exhausts me.

2:48 am – I GUESS WE BOTH HAVE ISSUES GETTING OUR POINTS ACROSS.

Julia wonders what he thought she tried to say.

June 7, 2012

1:39 am – Perry Thrust.

These words make her laugh, and as they seem to be an invitation, she responds in the darkness with: "Is that your porn name?"

Silence.

November 12, 2012

4:51 am – Everything tastes of gravel.

4:52 am – Looking at my life and the warrens in which I conceal myself.

4:53 am – I am not going to jump off a bridge.

She stares at that last message for a moment, considering what meaning he intends. Is he assuring her (and himself) that he is not going to kill himself? Or is he simply rejecting a particular option for suicide?

She decides he means the latter.

December 26, 2012

2:13 am – My plate is full as well.

2:14 am – Doggie bag ... paper plate?

2:15 am – I'll try the leftover hotline.

She recently read a short story which contained the line, "There is no way to know which is the last breath until the moment in which the possibility of appreciating the last breath has passed."

She takes a deep breath and goes to sleep.

April 3, 2013

4:41 am – I need you.

4:42 am – I need an hour of your time. An intelligent viewpoint. May I call you tomorrow?

4:43 am – No strings or depositions.

4:44 am – Just an ear to bend and two to listen?

4:56 am – please?

She hesitates but then texts back – "Yes. Call me tomorrow. "

5:19 am – Thank you, Julia.

The next day comes and goes without a call from him, as she knew it would.

June 26, 2013

3:38 am – I rebottled, took your first response to the cork.

5:52 am – The stench of failure permeates the offerings.

5:53 am – I completely understand.

As does she.

January 23, 2014

2:11 am – I have all my fingers, which gives me courage.

2:13 am – Flesh and bone attached.

2:14 am – I balk.

When they were children, he told her that it was as simple to bite off a finger as it was to bite through a carrot – he read it somewhere. The force required for both severings was the same, but the brain stopped you from biting through your own finger, that remnant of precluding self-preservation a proof of sanity, he said. She had never heard of this, and she was doubtful, pointing out that everyone they knew to be crazy in their own lives had all of their fingers.

"Yes," he said, "But if they wanted to bite them off, they could."

March 2, 2014

3:32 am – I am not going to walk into the ocean.

3:45 am – Run.

March 28, 2014

4:05 am – I need you. I am afraid. Are you there in the darkness?

4:06 am – Do you exist?

4:07 am – Do you ever ache for proof?

Julia stares at those last words, her fingers to her lips, touched.

Severed.

She wakes her husband at 4:13 am.

There is more blood than she expected.

Straw Man

"More?"

Without answering, Anna spread the fingers of her left hand and fanned them over the top of her half-filled cup. She was trying to pay attention to what he was saying, although even in their new arrangement, the words were familiar. Out of the corner of her eye, she saw the coffeepot rise and tip, and she glanced down at her hand, as though there was a possibility her fingers might have decided on their own to gesture beckoningly for more coffee. He was still talking, and so, stupidly, she doubled-down on her wordless demurral, spreading her right hand over her left, both hands over the cup.

Anna watched as the waitress poured the coffee through the sieve of her fingers.

"Damn it damn it damn it." She shook her hands in the air, flinging droplets of coffee everywhere. "Damn it."

He sank into silence as the waitress came to sudden life, resting the coffeepot on the table and wiping at the mess with a towel she pulled from her waistband. "I'm so sorry."

Anna dried her hands carefully with her napkin and inspected them. "It stings, that's all." She blew lightly across her skin, but before she could say, "I'm fine," the waitress was gone. Anna watched as the woman disappeared behind swinging doors, and then she stared at the doors, waiting for the waitress to return, perhaps with some ice, but after a few minutes, she realized that wasn't going to happen.

Across the table, Ben reached for the coffeepot, which the waitress had left behind. He refilled his cup and held the pot aloft. "You change your mind about the refill?"

"Seriously?"

He busied himself with peeling the tops off of tiny tubs of creamer. "I don't think she's coming back."

Anna shook her head in agreement and examined her hands again. The coffee must not have been that hot. Looking up at him, she held out her hands. "It hurts, but I'm fine. Thanks for asking."

He sipped his coffee, cocked his head. "Didn't I ask?"

"No."

"Sorry about that."

Anna sighed. She pressed the back of one hand and then the other against her glass of ice water. She returned her attention to him. "You were saying?"

He gathered himself up to continue, but then he slumped against the burnt-orange of the booth's vinyl seating and said nothing. It was as though her failed refusal had punctured him, and the words he might have spoken had escaped unnoticed in the moment of chaos, a hiss of meaningless air. She decided she would have a bit more coffee after all; she refilled her cup and lifted it to her lips. "I think I got the gist of it, but it really did seem like you had more to say."

He cocked his head at her again, this time assessingly. "No, I guess I was done."

She took a drink and then settled the cup on the tabletop. "It's nice to have the chance to talk without the girls. We should do this more often." He glanced at her, and she forced a laugh. "You know what I mean."

He scanned the room. "I really do think she's gone."

"The waitress, you mean? What does it matter? Did you want something?"

"No, it's just odd. She's not supposed to just fuck up and walk away."

She raised her eyebrows. "Maybe you should chase after her ... offer her that tip."

He returned his attention to his coffee.

Anna stared at her hands as she spoke. "Everyone has empty spaces. You're not special." He said nothing. She continued, her tone brighter, "Do you know you bring me here for the post-mortem every time? Five times now, altogether."

"That can't be right. Is that right?" He seemed to be doing some mental arithmetic as he spoke, and she could see that the numbers weren't adding up. She waited for him to realize that five was the number he'd shared with her and then she watched as his features smoothed into agreement. "I didn't realize we'd been here every time. I'm sorry."

"You're sorry about the uninspired restaurant selection?"

"What do you want me to say? I'm sorry about it all."

The waitress had done a shitty job of cleaning up the spill; Anna picked up her cup and settled it down in a small brown puddle. She picked her cup up again and then marched a line of coffee rings across her side of the table, watching the rings appear as if they held meaning. "When the girls were little, I used to tell them that the word 'sorry' was only meaningful if you then worked not to do the thing again. That you couldn't just keep making the same bad choice and trusting that *sorry* would make everything better." She slid her cup through the trail of rings, smearing the mess across the table. "At some point, I told them, you have to own that this is who you are and this is what you've done and this is what you will continue to do. There is no point to the apology, I told them, if the apology boils down to a mere acknowledgment that the other person does not appreciate your choices."

"But I am sorry."

She smiled. "That's what the girls used to insist as well."

"You have to understand ..."

"I do understand."

"I'm sorry."

There was a tumbler of paper-wrapped straws sitting alongside the condiment basket, and Anna reached for a straw. She played with it as she spoke. "Not so long ago, Jess asked me why I had married you, how I had known you were the one. At first I offered fragments of truth, the things parents say to curious children ... how we loved each other ... how we made one another happy ... how handsome I thought you were ... how I knew you were the one who could give her and her sister to me. Jess wasn't satisfied with those answers. She wanted, she said, to know about a moment when I saw you." Anna's voice grew hushed. "That's what she said ... she wanted to know about a moment when I saw you."

"What did you say?"

Instead of answering, Anna asked, "Do you remember once trying to impress me with the claim that you could break pencils with your bare hands?"

"Well, that makes it sound stupid," Ben protested, pleased to have been offered a change of conversation. "Anyone can break a pencil if they use both hands."

"Alright, *hand*. Remember? You splayed out the fingers of your right hand and threaded the pencil above just your middle finger ... below the fingers on either side. Remember? You said you could slam your hand down and break the pencil in two."

"Just for the record, I had broken pencils that way many times."

She smiled at the memory. "I was puzzled at your claim, because it was such a stupid thing to brag about ... such a weird way to try to impress me. But we were new, and I was prepared to ooh and ahh over broken pencils if that's what you had to offer, except then you slammed down your hand and the pencil didn't break."

He frowned. "I'm pretty sure they changed the wood formula for pencils, because there was a time I used to be able to snap pencils like matchsticks."

"Oh my god, it was amazing. Over and over, you slammed your hand against the table, and again and again the pencil refused to break. Your face was screwed up in pain, but you just kept readjusting the pencil between your fingers and explaining how the pencil must be defective."

"My hand hurt like hell." He thought back. "As I recall, you laughed like a crazy person."

"Because you wouldn't give up. Do you remember? It was such a stupid thing, and you wouldn't give up. I finally took pity on you and snatched the pencil away, snapping it in two with my hands."

"Yes, well ... both hands ... anyone can do that."

Anna grabbed another wrapped straw and handed it to him. "Do you remember the straw?"

Ben unwrapped the straw and threaded it above his middle finger and below the fingers on either side. "That's right! You handed me a straw and I snapped it right in two." He slammed his hand down on the table and the straw bent in the middle, its two ends shooting upward in surrender. "I crushed it. I can see why the memory lingered ... it was pretty impressive."

She unwrapped her own straw and held it up so that she could see through it. "No, what I remember most is how you filled the space. I remember looking at you through the length of a straw, and I remember your laughter and I remember the blue of your eyes and I remember the curve of your lips and I remember how you looked at me and I remember how you filled the space ... how you were everything."

"Through a straw."

"Yes, I know it sounds silly. But that moment, through a straw, as you laughed ... I saw you filling the spaces I hadn't even known to notice were empty."

He spoke quietly, "And that's what you told Jess?"

"Yes."

He fidgeted with the straw she'd given him, flattening it out and then tying it into a series of sharp-edged knots until it was a snarl of plastic. He tossed the end result on the table. "She didn't ask me if I saw you or how."

"If she had, though ... what would your answer have been?"

Ben opened his mouth as though to speak, but then he shook his head. "Never mind."

"Tell me."

He considered. "It was right before Claire was born, in the last moments of just the two of us."

She waited.

He spoke slowly. "It was early morning. You called my name. You called my name, and there was something about your voice –

something sharp and panicked. I knew this was it. I hurried to where you were. I was ready." He paused and reached to touch her hand, which hurt, and so she pulled away. She didn't bother explaining the pain. He stared down at his own empty hand. "I was so ready to be needed. You never seemed to need me."

She lifted the straw and stared at him through its tightened perspective as he continued.

"I hurried to you. You were standing at the window, your back to me, staring out at the field behind the house. You remember? You turned to me, and I remember the silhouette of your body, the exaggerated swell of your stomach. You turned to me and I reached for you, and your eyes were huge and dark, and you pointed a finger."

"I remember that," she whispered.

"I didn't understand at first. I thought the baby was coming, and so I didn't understand at first to look away and out the window."

"It was coming."

"I remember. A thick low fog, rolling in like the tide across the grass toward us. Faster and cleaner and sharper in its edges than I had ever seen fog, a roiling greedy thing of smoky gray, as wide as the world and as tall as the rooftops."

"I remember."

"You were terrified. You wanted me to stop it somehow. That's what you kept screaming ... *Make it stop!*" He picked up the knotted straw and fiddled with it. "And then you wanted to run."

Her voice was small as she agreed. "I wanted to outrun it. I tried to take your hand and drag you away. I remember."

"You were terrified. When I wouldn't come with you, you hung onto me and begged me to make it stop. It didn't even make sense, but I could see the fear was real to you."

Her voice flattened. "You didn't do anything."

"There was nothing I could do. You started crying. Over and over and over you demanded I make it stop. I tried to reassure you, but you were hysterical, so I just held you tight. I held you tight and we stared out the window as the fog rolled in and over us and stole the world."

She stared through the straw at his face. "Yes."

"The whole thing, from the moment I heard you call my name to gray surrender, took maybe three minutes, and afterward, nothing was the same."

She closed her eyes.

He reached again for her hand, and in the darkness, she pulled away again. His voice was softer now. "It's true. I saw you."

She took a deep breath. "That's the moment you choose? That's what you would have told Jess?"

"I didn't tell Jess. I'm telling you."

She opened her eyes and stared into his. "I am just so tired of the telling."

Startled by the hostility in her tone, he drew back. "You asked me to share a moment."

"I suppose I did." She shook her head. "It's too much."

"What is, exactly?"

"Everything. You and whoever she is this time, comparing stories and holes, poking one another's fingers into the empty spaces and calling it a fit. It's too much." Her voice rose. "Sitting in this same booth listening to your same secrets – it's too much. Not once ...

not twice ... but over and over again. I don't remember agreeing to
do this. I don't know how I have come to do this."

He was silent.

Anna continued. "Your story of the fog ..." She reached with both
hands to gather her long hair and tie it in a messy knot at the
nape of her neck. "It sounds crazy, right? Pregnancy fucks with a
woman's emotions, intensifies them ... but ... and this is
important, Ben ... it doesn't make the underlying truth any less
real." Anna brought her hands back to her face, spoke through the
spaces among her fingers. "It wasn't fog. It was real and it
changed everything, and you did nothing to stop it."

"What are you talking about?" He sat back and arranged his
features into puzzlement. "It was fog. I saw it, and how was I
supposed to stop it?"

"Oh, for fuck's sake." Her fingers still covered her mouth, but her
voice was louder now, and angry. "Just because you didn't think
to get us a booth back then doesn't mean it didn't happen."

"Anna, we have been through this."

"No. Not this. We've been through a lot of things, but we have
never been through this. You will not sit there and suggest that
my request you turn back the fog changed everything. I asked you
to make it stop and you did not."

"I'm confused."

"Are you?" She glared at him in challenge. "What was her name?
The woman who plays the role of fog in your story ... what was her
name?" She saw realization dawn in his eyes. "Yes. Her. The
woman who lingered in the background of our new marriage like
mist. I stood there in the kitchen, the night before our baby was
born, looking out the window as the mist became a living
breathing thing, a woman who solidified and muscled into my life,
into my marriage, into my future. She was real."

Anna took a deep shuddering breath and swallowed hard against the pain. "Don't you dare suggest there was a moment in which everything could have been different, but then I asked the impossible and ruined it all. Don't you dare. I needed you. More than I have ever needed anyone in my life, I needed you. I turned to you. I asked you to make it stop and I asked you to save us, and I asked you to take my hand and run away with me, and instead ..."

His voice was a whisper. "I didn't know you knew. You didn't say."

"Instead you gathered me in your arms and ... how did you put it? *You held me tight and we stared out the window as the fog rolled in and stole the world.*"

"I'm so sorry. I didn't know you knew."

"Yes, well ... I didn't know it was possible to build a life on the sand of unsaid and unmeant, but here we are. Look what we have done, Ben. Look what we have made. Pour me another cup, Ben. Tell me a story; the endings are my favorite part. Apologize again for the broken promises. Offer me again the death of a wanting that is not for me. Let me cradle that corpse in my palms and tell you that I understand."

They sat in silence for a moment, sipping at the dregs of now-cold coffee.

Anna ended the quiet. "We've done this together."

"What?"

"How did I not know?" She waved her hands as he started to protest. "No, I know what you've been doing. I mean ... I didn't see. I refused to see."

"What do you mean?"

She spoke softly now, her voice gentle. "All this time, you've been trying to show me you can break the thing you hold." She shook her head wonderingly. "I've been accepting apologies for the wrong failure." She reached for another straw and unwrapped it. "Let me make this easier."

"Anna."

"Shhh ...." She threaded the straw beneath the middle finger of his right hand and then rested the ache of her hand atop his. "Look at the trick we can do with love."

A waitress appeared – a different waitress – and she frowned at the empty coffeepot on their table. She looked at them both and held her fresh coffeepot up in halfhearted offer. "I don't suppose you want any more?"

"No."

Alight briefly

Her lower right side hurt again. Indigestion, maybe. Or cancer. Or a blood clot. Or the early symptom of some other horrific diagnosis that would become official too late for anything to be done. The doctor would shake his head sadly as he consulted her charts. Didn't you, he would ask, notice any symptoms? Fuck you, she would say, and then by way of coy apology, she would admit to a certain lowering of inhibitions. She wondered if there were doctors who found dying irresistible, if that was even a thing. She shifted painfully. She knew one thing – if she *was* dying, she was going to take up smoking.

In the moments after her hands were emptied, she had never known what to do with them. Or rather, she knew what to do with her hands, but everyone knew smoking killed you ... everyone knew that. Except, somehow, despite the fact that she didn't smoke and had never smoked, once her hands were empty, she was a smoker. Her hands retained some past-life memory of the rituals and the movements and the toxic claiming of the space around her body. Her hands yearned for purpose in the moments in-between that were her life.

And so she had promised herself that when she knew she was dying, she would take up smoking. In a weird way, she looked forward to the ritual of departing by slightly hastened degrees. *Six months? Fuck your six months. Got a light? I'll be out of here in four.*

She was going to be seriously irritated if she ended up being taken out by a bus.

Damn, her side hurt. She bent slightly and pressed her fingers hard into the pain. She wished David was here, but he was gone of course, and even before he died, he hadn't really been here. Sometimes, after a few drinks, she would inform people that she'd been married for 27 years, widowed for four, and that she had missed her husband every day for the past 30 years.

That first year had been good.

Still, if he was here, he would tell her to stop whining and he would tell her to stop eating so much shit she was getting fat and no wonder she had indigestion and he would tell her to stop pissing all over his weekend. For christ's sake, he would say, you're not dying.

If David was here, she could take comfort in his dismissive certainty. She pressed her fingers hard into the pain again. Of course, David had been completely unaware of his own impending death, even as the others announced the countdown, so maybe he wasn't to be trusted in such matters.

Tell that motherfucking cocksucking prick of a nurse he can take his catheter and shove it up his ass, he said, and then he cackled wildly.

As last words went, she supposed those weren't bad.

She bent over as far as she could, jamming both of her fists into the jagged softness of the pain. It was apparent from this position that the carpet needed cleaning, and she took a deep breath and exhaled the thought into words to test the boundaries of the agony. The words escaped on currents of deflation as she folded farther upon herself. "Need to rent one of those carpet-cleaners."

She waited a moment then, folded over and breathless.

Just in case there was time to have better last words than ones referencing dirty carpeting, she quickly whispered the ones she had prepared. "I alight briefly and am gone."

The pain began to subside.

She unfolded herself slowly, cautiously, but whatever the problem had been, it appeared to have resolved itself, at least for now. To be certain, she stretched this way and that, searching for the pain, but all she found was the lingering corrosive shrill of fear. Her skin was slick with sweat and her mouth was raw and tasted of metal's filth, as though she had been licking a screen door.

Into the cavern the pain had made of her plans for the day spread the overwhelming urge to go for a walk. Going for a walk was so out of character for her that at first, she tried to compromise by walking around the house. The house was small, so this walking was accomplished in short order and did nothing to abate the desire. Resigned and also curious, she walked out to the sidewalk in front of her house, wondering where she was going.

Her feet went left and she went with them.

As she walked, her arms swung at her sides, her hands clenched around a wish.

It was a lovely warm day, and she had the world to herself. Having nothing else to do as she walked, she stared down and avoided stepping on the many cracks in the sidewalk, humming the back-breaking song as she went. There was no one left to save, but it seemed the least she could do.

So intent was she on avoiding cracks, she caught up with and then almost ran into the naked man.

Stopping her song and her endeavors, she took inventory as he continued his journey uninterrupted, slowly walking away from her. He wasn't actually completely naked. He wore a loose blue t-shirt and a gray baseball cap. On his feet were sandals of some sort, and puddled around his ankles were his pants.

He was very thin, shockingly thin, the sort of thin in which all buffers have been eaten away, a thin whose falling meant breaking. He moved, she thought, with an exaggerated stiffness and fragility, as though he was walking on the lengths of a wishbone. She rubbed fingers against her thumb, remembering the childhood pull and then the snap of dry bone in pursuit of wishes. No more wishes for this man, she thought, and she wondered how rapid had been the weight loss that the pants now around his ankles were his.

She considered, wondering what help she might be able to offer and if it would be welcome. Standing still, she watched him walk away in slow stilted motion; where was he going? It was going to take him forever to get there. What if he tripped on his pants and snapped into pieces? What if someone else saw him and called the police?

Still, how was she supposed to initiate a conversation?

Pardon me, sir ... I was walking along avoiding the cracks when I almost fell into yours.

OK, yes ... she could say that.

She hurried to catch up to him and then took a few more steps to pass him and block his path. She turned back to face him and said, "Excuse me, sir ... I ..." and then she stopped, because now she was facing the front of a very thin naked man, and she had obviously not thought this all the way through.

She dragged her eyes up to his face, which was just as weathered and loose as what hung below – she guessed he was close to 75. She searched for words and came up with, "Lucy," which was her name, and she extended her hand. When he said nothing, but instead just stared at her, she repeated herself. "Lucy." She reached forward slightly with her extended hand, curving her fingers a bit and moving her hand slightly to demonstrate the handshake she was inviting.

At which point, she realized for the first time in her life that the initiation of a handshake relied heavily on the other person wearing clothing, especially if the effort was to go unrequited. Because now she was standing just a few feet away from a half-nude man with her hand reaching for his limp dick, and worse, she was still pantomiming a handshake – why was she doing that? – she looked for all the world like she was offering to jack him off.

Regretting everything, she pulled her hand back and pinned it to her side. Smiling, she said again, "Lucy."

He stared at her. She repeated her name again. Like a goddamned idiot. Her eyes slid down his body, and she realized her name sounded like loosey and was not helping the situation at all. Damn it.

She tried again. "My name is Lucy."

Something like humor flickered in his eyes, and she took this as a good sign. "Yes, my name is Lucy, and I couldn't help noticing that you seem to have gone out into the world half ..." Oh my god, she meant to say *half-dressed* but she had almost said *half-cocked*. What was wrong with her? She sighed and threw her arms up in a gesture of helplessness. "Your pants. You're not wearing them."

There was silence except for exhaustion, and she realized then he had been using the awkwardness of her one-sided introductions to surreptitiously regain his breath. He looked so frail and overwhelmed that she was surprised at the depth and strength of his voice when he said simply, "I am aware."

"So ... ummm ... is this a choice you've made intentionally?"

He took a few more rasping breaths and shrugged his shoulders. "Nope."

"Perhaps a belt?"

"I used to have a belt. Don't know what happened to it." He leaned forward to rest his hands on his bare thighs and was silent again as he breathed deeply. When he had regained his composure, if not his pants, he straightened, met her eyes. "She probably took it, just in case."

"Just in case what? And anyway, you can't go around with your pants around your ankles."

"I find that I can, albeit slowly," he assured her.

"You're telling me you walk around like this all the time?"

"No," he admitted. "She likes me to stay where she can see me, but today, I needed the river, and so I left."

"She?"

He waved his hand as though to swat a fly. "What does it matter? There is always a she, and she always has opinions and she always has control."

Glancing around, she realized they were only a few blocks from the river. She turned back to him. "Here's the thing. Earlier, I thought I was dying and then I was not, and then I was overcome by the need to walk but not around my house because I tried that and I have never known what to do with my hands not once since my daughter died and so I have no idea what I am doing and guidance would be much appreciated and why aren't you wearing any underwear?"

He glanced down. "I've never been a fan of confinement." She snorted with laughter, and he went on, "You thought you were dying; I am actually dying. Not today, perhaps, but soon, they tell me, and on a day not of my choosing. I woke today consumed by the need for the river, but it's been a while since I have done anything more adventurous than wait. My pants don't fit and she took my belt because it tightens too well. I am tired. I need help." He glared at her and spoke fiercely, "I don't want help."

She took a step backward, ready to end the conversation, but the glare hadn't been for her, because he added, more softly, "Would you please help me?"

She bent beside him and pulled his pants to his knees as he rested a hand on her shoulder. Gently, she tugged the pants up around his waist as he sank against her. The pants were very loose, frighteningly loose, and there was no way they were going to stay up without assistance. Still holding the waistband of his pants, she asked, "Can you hold them up as you walk?"

"I thought so, but you see how well that worked out." His voice quavered. "I get scared I will fall, and I need my hands to brace against the nothing. Please?"

"Alright, so we'll walk together." She wrapped her left arm around him and hooked a finger through the belt-loop at his side. Her right hand, she crossed over her body to hook another finger through the belt-loop between their bodies. "I think that if you lean into me a bit, we can make this work." They took a few tentative steps together, and soon fell into a slow but steady rhythm. "I am still Lucy, by the way."

His hand rested above the curve of her hip and flattened itself against the memory of pain. "My name is Edward."

"Nice to meet you, Edward. I would shake your hand, but my hands are busy."

Having dispensed with the need for a handshake, he skipped the pleasantries of small-talk as well. "When did your daughter die?"

She pretended to be so occupied with finding the proper balance that words were impossible. She wasn't going to answer, she wasn't going to say another word, and then she surprised herself by saying, "Thirty years ago this week." She paused. "And thank you."

"For what?"

"For not prefacing your question with the phrase *Forgive me for asking, but …* . The question that follows those words is always painful enough; the requirement that I forgive the pain is excruciating."

He said, "Not so hard …" and she relaxed her grip on him, realizing a few steps later that wasn't what he'd meant.

They walked a little farther, until the sidewalk gave way to the bright green of grass and the darker green of water, and then they sat together in the shade beneath a tree. He leaned back on his elbows, exhausted by the journey, his breath labored and ragged. She was tired as well; by the end, she had been holding up his body as well as his pants. After a few minutes, it occurred to her that she was lingering uninvited in his moment, and she started to stand, to apologize, "I'll leave you to …" but he patted her hand and looked at her for a moment before turning his gaze back to the river.

"I want to hear the story."

She sat back down and ripped at the grass on either side of her, tangled the small green lengths in her fingers and pulled them free, dropped their messy confetti of surrender in her lap. Finally, she asked, "What story?"

He leaned his head back and closed his eyes. "The story you clutch in your fists."

"You don't know what I hold."

He nodded slightly, agreeing. "Wouldn't be much of a story if I'd heard it before."

By way of delaying, she challenged him, wanting to make him as uncomfortable as she felt in this moment. "You said you were dying. What do you have?"

But he only laughed softly, his eyes still closed. "All the time in the world."

Extending her arm, she swept her fingers over the river and the hills beyond, relinquishing perspective until everything was small.

I was an only child. I was seven years old, and Christmas was coming. I had asked for a bicycle, because even though it was winter and would be winter for months to come, my birthday wasn't until late in August, and I had plans to spend the entire summer riding that bicycle. My parents didn't have much money, and there were few opportunities to ask for something extra, and so that Christmas, I asked only for the bicycle – just the one thing. Several weeks before Christmas, my parents started taking the early evenings to meet in secret. They needed to work on my present, they said. My father installed two small locks high on the guest-room door, one on the inside and one on the outside, and every evening after dinner, they would retreat to this room and work on my gift.

At first, I was fine with being left out, because I really wanted that bicycle, and I figured bicycles took some time to assemble. After several nights of being all alone, however, I started to wonder what could be taking so long, and so I listened at the door. I heard them laughing and whispering and working together; they sounded so happy and so unlike the parents I knew. It was wonderful and also a little bit scary, because as the nights went on and the secret happiness continued, I felt more and more excluded.

After the eighth or ninth night, I couldn't take it anymore. As I listened to them laughing and talking quietly, I began to pound on the door. I whined and cried and begged for them to let me in on the secret. I laid on the floor and kicked my heels on the door as I chanted, "Let … me … in."

There was silence in the room, and then the door opened, just a crack, and my mother peered out at me. "Lucy," she said, "We are working on your Christmas present. We need time to make it perfect. Your father and I are sacrificing our time to give this to you, and we do not want to hear from you again."

That quieted me for a few more days, but I couldn't help wonder how much work a bicycle could possibly be. I began to leave possible behind; I began to imagine impossible instead ... bicycles that flew high in the air or dove under water or made me invisible. This bicycle was going to change everything.

I sat on the couch alone and dreamed. They worked in secret every night, these parents who laughed and sang and were different than I had ever known. This time together had clearly become the best part of their day. They moved the radio in with them and played music. My mother prepared drinks and snacks. Somehow, all their words, when I listened, were whispers.

They never forgot to lock the door.

By the time Christmas morning arrived, the thing I wanted most in the world was not the bicycle, but the secret's end.

Their faces ... I still remember their faces. I remember the mixture of pride and joy and hopefulness. Of vulnerability. I remember the vulnerability, and I remember the fragility of the moment as they stepped aside to reveal my gift.

It was a dollhouse.

It was a huge wooden dollhouse, taller than I was, painstakingly assembled from thousands of pieces. It was exquisite in every detail, and every perfectly decorated room was filled with perfectly crafted miniature furniture. They pulled me close and, our three heads together, they pointed out the details I might have missed ... the glitter-painted silver chandelier; the tiny braids of the yarn rug; the wallpaper cut from scraps of paper they'd collected; the aluminum foil pressed into tiny frames to serve as mirrors; the fingernail-sized stuffed pillows on the beds; the carefully folded piles of gossamer linens. There were things they'd purchased already made as well ... little bathtubs and sinks and a toilet and a fireplace that actually lit, its warm glow emanating from the tiniest of light-bulbs. They reached their out-of-proportion hands to show me how the doors opened and the drawers slid and the beds unmade. With giddy voices, they *spilled the secrets of their time together, how they had made this ... all of this ... for me.*

I tried. For a moment, I tried. "Where," I asked, "is the family who lives here?"

They looked at me in puzzlement. My father shook his head. "The house is for you."

It was more than I could take. I watched their faces crumple as I screamed my pent-up frustration and loneliness and betrayal. "This present is not for me! I don't fit in it! This is what you've been doing? This is what you thought I would love? I don't even play with dolls. Not ever. You thought I wanted to be one? This is the dumbest present ever! I wanted a bicycle! I hate you. I hate this dollhouse and I hate you! I hate you! I hate you!"

Whatever broke that day, it never mended.

Or maybe it had always been broken, but now, through a tiny window of stained-glass candy-wrapper translucency, we saw.

When she was done talking, they sat together and watched the unchanging river as it changed endlessly.

He reached to rest the frailty of his hand on hers. "When I was a child, I wished on stars."

She turned to him. "Yes?"

"I wished on stars, every wish the same, a wish for less."

"Less?"

"Less hurt, less anger, less bitterness, less fear, less futility."

"I see."

He nodded. "One night, my father saw me lying in the grass, wishing on stars, and he sat beside me, demanded an explanation, which I gave. I will never forget what he said then ... he said, 'A star is just the fire of destruction's promise. You're wishing on the promise of an end.' And then he stood up, wiped his pants and towered over me for a second in the darkness, the glow of his cigarette brightening as he inhaled and dimming as he exhaled the words against the smoke. 'Good luck with that, boy.'"

"From then on, I wished on cigarettes." Edward bent forward to dump his baseball cap from his head, and he retrieved from its hollow a pack of cigarettes and a lighter. He lit one for himself and then extended the pack to her. "The only hiding place I have left to me." His eyes sparkled. "Each one is a small fire of destruction's promise." He inhaled deeply to brighten the fire and then spoke around the smoke, "Each one's a star ... but less."

She slid a cigarette from the pack and placed it between her lips, leaning forward into his cupped hands to catch ignition. "You still make the same wish?"

"It's the wish we all make, in the end."

They smoked companionably, her fingers dancing destruction's promise as though by rote.

Curious, she asked, "Why did you need the river today?"

He raised his eyebrows, as though surprised at her question. "She took my belt."

She let that truth settle for a moment. "You're going to wait for darkness?"

"I thought so, yes. First, because a man who cannot walk without losing his pants needs cover of darkness for secret undertakings, and second ..."

She finished for him. "The stars will be out."

"Indeed." He lay on his back in the grass, folded his baseball cap and wedged it beneath his head, and closed his eyes. "I may take a nap until the evening arrives."

The last thing he said was like an afterthought, and he raised his hand slightly to get her attention, his eyes still closed. "What was her name, the girl who did not fit in the house you made for her?"

She couldn't remember the last time she had spoken it aloud. "Lona."

He nodded slightly and let his hand fall to the ground. Soon he was asleep.

She sat there for a while, watched as the day turned to dusk.

As the light faded, she lit another cigarette and made a quiet wish on its promised end.

I alight briefly and am gone.

Destruction blazed and filled her lungs.

I ... alight ... briefly ...

and am gone.

Robin's-egg blue

The bicycle shifted in the back of the minivan, a grinding metallic protest that cut through the emotion that drove her away. With reluctance, she allowed herself to be detoured into memory; she swung hard around the next few turns of road to listen for the sound again, to gauge its quality. Too fast for the small bridges over small canals of this small town of fingered water, she spun the wheel and listened. It was a strange fierce sound, like something under pressure giving just enough to hold. She searched through what she knew for the knowledge, and arrived below the water.

Below the water of another's imagination, within a short story she had read months before about a Civil War submarine; the author had described the sound of metal adjusting to the changes of depth's pressure as "the tallying of implausibility."

The tallying of implausibility ...

She was 48 years old, making her getaway in a minivan along tiny leafy streets over tiny carved waterways with a child's carelessly thrown bicycle speaking to her of the improbability of survival.

Life was ludicrous.

A delivery truck of some sort appeared in front of her, lumbering slowly. Too slowly, hugging the right side of the tree-lined street, the driver probably looking for an address. She settled in behind the truck, close enough that the truck disappeared; her vision filled with the blank flatness of metal painted white.

Against the huge rectangle of the truck's back doors, her memory flickered the filmstrip of hurt, a stop-motion replay of her face in extreme close-up as truths washed over like the rising tide. From this perspective, hands on the wheel, she could see the drowning as it unfolded onscreen; it was almost beautiful – the water softened her features, eroded the structure of adulthood, wavered the boundaries of pain and love ... breath and death ... wanting and need. With each new depth, she watched as she inhaled the heavy liquid of a life collapsed, relinquishing her hold on equilibrium.

anguish
fear
sorrow
guilt
vulnerability
grief
despair

They hurt her so easily.

They had no idea how easily she could hurt.

It was the one thing she could give them.

It was the one thing she could keep from them.

On the screen of recent past, her features coalesced and hardened and emerged, sending ripples across the surface of their cruelties.

rage

She heard the sound of her fingers gathering keys in a jumble of escape.

flight

The bicycle shifted again as she followed the truck around another corner. The trees hung into the street here, and the truck swept its upper right angles through the untrimmed branches. The white blankness against which she had projected now revealed itself to be the outlines of something massive and unseen. As the truck imposed itself, the branches bent and tensed and held, whipping the air before her as they swung back into position.

A thousand leafy catapults, empty but for one.

The eggs shattered bright blue against her windshield; she never saw them fly. Jeweled blue starbursts surrounded twin deaths, the tiny beings crushed by the impact into a sodden mess of blood and yolk and bone. Proof of their undone lives dripped through her vision as she drove.

She wondered if they registered the tallying of implausibility.

Wondered if they knew to listen.

She took a deep breath and swung the car for home.

There was no way to ask without revealing herself.

As pages turn

The pool is enclosed, and its wall of windows looks out on the ocean, or it did at one time. Now, the exterior of the glass is etched and scrawled by endless sand-blown gusts, and the interior is fogged with the damp humidity of sweltered flesh and bleach. Along the wall, there is a long wooden bench, and it is on this bench her husband sits, fully dressed, reading a magazine. She swims back and forth across the pool, which is small and shallow, trying to work out what's caught her attention, and then she realizes – he has left his phone behind, afraid to expose it to the chemical-laden steam of this warmed room of water. She tries to remember the last time she saw him without his phone; even when he is asleep, it is on his bedside table – it's the first thing he reaches for when he wakes. Now she watches as he turns a page, and she flips away and under.

Once, long ago, when they were newly married, she sat on a couch and wept, for reasons she cannot recall. From the other room, she heard the sounds of her husband ignoring her tears, which altered the course of her sadness – she began to weep about her isolation, upset with him for avoiding her need. When he finally appeared in the doorway, she was startled by the look of frustration on his face, and his words lowered her expectations, one by one. "I am a separate person," he informed her, "I am here, but I am not going to be able to be *here*," and he waved his hands in her direction, "at your emotional beck and call. I am in this house and I will always be here, but you are going to have to do the work of you," and he paused to sigh, as though exhausted at the mere contemplation of all the work she might require, "by yourself."

There are words that linger, and then there are words that stain the future resting beyond their utterance.

She breaks the surface of the water as pages turn.

He arranged this weekend without explanation, a borrowed timeshare in a small oceanside development. Built in 1963, the development's maintenance and upkeep since then seems to have consisted of little more than the stewardship and acceptance of eventual ruination. The timeshare owners she has seen during their visit thus far appear to be of similar philosophy, their bodies large and soft, their pale overripe flesh mottled with bruises and snaked with the darkness of vesseled surrender, their skin runnelled with the scars of burdens carried and lost and carried further still. She is about twenty years younger than they are, young enough to have been the child upon whose floating body they once rested gentle fingers of reassurance just as she once rested gentle fingers of reassurance against the tentatively buoyant flesh of her own children.

"I'm right here."

The thing about children she never appreciated until they left was simply ... that they left.

Back and forth she swims as pages turn.

. . . .

Outside, the ocean is gray and cold and angry, its waves froth-crested with a yellow-green foam that rides the water to the sand and hulks in shimmering clots of malignity. Yesterday, she walked along the water's edge, careful to avoid the foam, thinking it was pollution of some sort. When she got back to the development, she stopped by the lobby to ask the woman behind the desk about the foam, and she learned she was half-right – it was algae, whipped up by the frenzied water, but the algae itself was blooming in excessive amounts, its growth fueled by radioactivity released into the ocean by a nuclear meltdown in faraway Japan. The woman shook her head. "Nuclear radiation is carried on the currents, and when it arrives on our shores, the algae reaches for the energy it can synthesize into food. Nuclear, solar ... algae doesn't distinguish between types of radiation. If the energy comes from below and sideways and all around instead of from up above, the algae doesn't care. It just reaches for nourishment ... blooms in the poison."

Was this true? She didn't know. It felt true.

They went out to dinner, her husband and she, at a lovely restaurant overlooking the calm waters of the ocean-linked bay. As they sipped their drinks and considered the menu, chunks of what looked like Styrofoam began to float across the water toward them. Big solid-looking chunks, some as large as picnic coolers, bobbed on the water, attracting the attention of the room's diners and causing some consternation until the wait-staff explained it was just algae, churned up by the ocean and sent floating into calmer connected waters. A good thing, their waitress explained – it meant the water was full of nutrients.

Remembering her earlier discussion about radioactivity and meltdowns and blooms of poison, she found herself unable to order any of the seafood dishes. She tried to find her appetite, but in the end, she settled for a small salad and bread.

Her husband, who had chosen the restaurant, was annoyed with her order, and he leaned across the table to wonder why she always had to be where he wasn't. "Why," he asked, "Are we never on the same page?" She stared at him as he returned his attention to his menu, seemingly unaware that he had just summed up the question of their life together in a single handful of words. Caught off guard by the depth of the sadness his question elicited, she attempted to apologize by ordering another drink and laughing at his stories, which she knew by rote.

Sex she also offered by way of apology, by rote, and then she lay awake in the darkness, the ocean's roar a heralded metronome of distant disaster thudding against the membranes that separated her from sleep.

. . . .

Surface tension yields as pages turn.

Her husband closes his magazine and stands, walking along the pool's edge as she swims until she stops to look up at him. He gestures vaguely to indicate departure. "I have to go out. I have some work to do ... some people to meet ... a couple of hours." He pats at his pocket to indicate his phone as he says, "Just got a call – something's come up." She watches as his hand pats at nothing but the small lie. When she says nothing in response, he shrugs his shoulders. "Maybe when you're done swimming, you could take a walk along the beach. I'll meet up with you for lunch."

She nods, knowing there is no point in asking him to change plans he hasn't even made.

A short while later, she is standing on the beach, showered and changed, her damp hair tucked beneath a knit cap, a jacket zipped up against the windy chill. She stands facing the ocean for a moment, and then she turns left and walks along its edge, avoiding the foam. She walks for quite a while, pausing occasionally to examine bits of shell or broken shards of sand dollar, and then she comes to a small stream running into the ocean from the woods just beyond the beach's sand. It's too large a stream for her to cross without getting her shoes and pants wet; she decides to track it up toward its source, hoping to find a way across. As she nears the woods, the stream widens into a small rocky pond, and in its farthest corner, she is surprised to see a man standing in the water, holding a long thick branch. Beside him is a seal, lying listlessly in the shallow pool, its gray coat dappled with silver, its chubby body almost cartoonish in its roundness.

"Came up with the tide last night. Beached herself," the man offers by way of explanation as he pushes the end of the branch he is holding beneath the seal's head. "Thought at first she came up to find a place to have her baby. They do that sometimes, but this mama's lost her baby somewhere, and she's sick."

She takes a few steps closer. The seal doesn't move, but its eyes follow her approach. "You know about seals?"

"Yes, ma'am. She's not going to make it, I'm afraid."

"Shouldn't we call someone?"

He laughs a brief humorless laugh. "I'm the one who's been called. There's nothing to do but make her comfortable, keep people and dogs from bothering her."

"She looks pregnant ... you sure she's not?"

He meets her eyes. "Yes ma'am. We ran some bloodwork early this morning. She was pregnant recently, but she isn't now. Not much to be done. She's got a sickness that's been hitting a lot of the seals and sea lions lately."

"Can't you ..."

She lets the question fade away, and he nods his head. "Thing is, the only thing keeping her alive at the moment is this branch. I've been holding her head up out of the water for the past half hour or so." As he finishes speaking, he repositions the branch, wedging it in the rocks and sand beneath the seal's chin and then using the leverage to pull the seal's face free of the water. The animal stares up at them, her eyes soft and brown and tired.

"There's no way to save her?"

"Truth be told, the kindest thing would be to lay this branch down, which I was just about to do when you walked up."

"You don't have a faster way?"

"I can arrange for a faster way, but the faster way won't get here in time."

They stare at the seal for a few moments, and then she walks into the water to stand beside the man. She bends to stroke a finger along the animal's flank. She whispers, "I'm right here." The seal's flesh shudders, a shivering ripple as though of fever, and then it stills beneath her caress. The man pulls the support away, and the seal's head lolls and sinks into the water. She continues to run soothing fingers along its sleek fur, continues to whisper, "I'm right here."

The seal's eyes shut and then open and then go blank. There are some bubbles, but not many. She rests a hand against dappled silver and continues to whisper reassurance. Tears swell in her eyes.

There is a silence then, and after the silence has passed, she stands and takes a deep breath. "I should get back."

"Yes, ma'am." He pauses, as though trying to find the words he wants, settling finally for a helpless kind of, "Thank you."

She hurries back, cold and wet, but instead of changing for lunch, she strips off her clothes, pulls on her still sodden bathing suit, and heads to the warmth of the pool. The pool is empty except for her, and she swims back and forth as she thinks. Back and forth she swims until he comes to find her, annoyed to have his plans disrupted. "What are you doing? I said I would meet you for lunch."

She spins in the water to float on her back, and instead of answering him, she asks, "Did you know it is possible to bloom in poison and never know that's what you've done?"

He stares at her.

With her hands, she carves small figure-eights in the water as she floats. "Did you know it is possible to live a life nourished by unintentional harm?"

"What are you talking about?"

She spins to face him, treading water. "Let's do this."

"Do what, exactly?"

She meets his eyes, meets the confusion she sees in them. She almost laughs; even these last moments together will be done alone. She lifts her chin high above the water, certain of her words. "Yes, let's do this now."

Cinereality

She sits, too early by far, in the parking lot outside the silent gray brick of the walls that hold her future. Neatly aligned between the parallels, she stares through the window without seeing, her eyes numb to the details of the passage of moments her mother used to call "sameless." She looks backward into memory to find the difference.

. . . . .

Her mother's hair is a curtain of rust, her mother's eyes the frozen blue of deep water beneath thin ice, her skin the freckled map of all the places ever dreamed. When her mother speaks, her hands caress unseen music in the spaces between her words. "Nothing is the same as it has ever been. Each moment is everything ... for just that moment. Each moment passes into the next, and the next is not the same." Her mother smiles. "Each moment is sameless, never to be repeated and impossible to hold."

She is a serious little girl, and so she nods, entranced but also frightened of the seeming obligations involved in seeing what there is to see in every moment that arrives.

She is overwhelmed at the thought of all the moments that will never be again.

. . . . .

Again.

Brushing tears from her eyes, she reaches for the moment in which she rests, reaches to angle the rear-view mirror so that she might stare unseeing into its reflection. She doesn't need to see to know. Her hair is the color of frosted rust. Her eyes are a shallow frozen blue. Her face is freckled with nightmare. Her hands clutch at the single mourning note that winds its way through her every exhalation.

She is her mother repeated, but without the magic. Without the same.

Sighing, she allows her vision to drift beyond the outlines of silver-backed glass to the world beyond, her attention caught by the movement of leaves as they fall from the trees through windless silhouetting clarity. It is mid-January, and across the parking lot, a perfect line of small branched trees hold their naked arms up against the cinereal sky.

She checks the time. Still early. Lately all they do is argue, and she has no desire to be early to confrontation.

The leaves fall from the trees.

She sits and rubs her hands together as the warmth of the car surrenders and cedes to the world's chill. Winter here in Oregon is a weighty damp gray that settles like ashen moss on the convolutions of her brain, eating at the surfaces and increasing the spans across which synapses must fire. She loves Oregon, but the winters make her weak.

The leaves fall from the empty trees.

Wait.

The leaves fall from a single tree ... a single solitary dancer performing an unexpected bit of fluttering poetry against the stark.

Just one tree, one tree in the middle of the line of small identical trees, has held its leaves beyond the season.

She stares as the tree hurls its leaves to the ground, spitting them from its branches as though suddenly embarrassed to be caught out in stubborn refusal to relinquish. This casting out and down continues for perhaps ten seconds, until the tree stands identical to its neighbors, bare before the world, not a single leaf upon its branches. She stares, not sure what to make of what she has witnessed.

The trees stand now in an obedient row, naked against the muted silver sky.

She stares.

The trees stand naked.

Sometimes there is no explanation.

It's still early.

She leans her head back and closes her eyes, remembering the words of the nurse after her last visit ...

. . . . .

"You upset him with your insistence that he remember everything as you do. He's not trying to antagonize you; he remembers what he remembers; there's no hostility in his mistakes." The nurse took her hand to soften the scolding. "It is kinder to listen and accept his memories for what they are ... versions of the truth."

She nodded her head, because there was no explanation she wanted to offer this woman.

The truth is that when her father gets lost in a misremembered past, it feels as though he is erasing his life as well as hers ... as though he is undoing the truths of their history. The house on Overlook Lane had been blue, not green; they moved to Indiana when she was nine, not eleven; the dog had been named Benjamin, not Brandy. Her mother died in the spring, not the winter; her mother's hair was not red and her eyes were not grey and she did not love him, not when it counted.

She cannot seem to help herself; she catalogs and corrects his mistakes. Her every correction angers him. "It doesn't matter what I say. Listen to me." He fixes glittering eyes on her as he takes her hand and pulls her close. "Listen to the me in what I say."

That doesn't even make sense, and she tells him so as she pulls away.

He extends a pleading hand into the space from which she withdraws. "You look just like your mother."

"No, Dad. No, I do not."

"Where is she, anyway? She promised she would visit me today."

"Mom's gone, Dad. She died a long long time ago."

His face crumples, but then he shakes his head. "No, that's not right. She was here yesterday. She held my hand and we sang a song about the moon."

"That was me, Dad."

He's confused. "Was it?" And then he smiles. "Stay until she gets here so I can take a picture of the two of you together." She says nothing, and he looks out the window and continues as though his next sentence follows sensibly from the last, "She died in the winter once, when I was leaving."

She died in the spring.

If the past is nothing more than shared truth, his relinquishment of this obligation both infuriates and terrifies her.

. . . . .

A single tree stands and spreads its leafy branches in search of sun.

Wait.

From this distance and in this light, the tree and its leaves are shades of black and gray, but she sees the rustling movement of the leaves against a slight breeze. The same tree that threw its garments to the ground just a few moments before is now once again clothed. For that one tree, the rules of time and season seem to have been held in abeyance.

How can that be?

She stares without blinking, willing the tree to throw its leaves again, and when it does, she sees what she did not see before.

The leaves are not leaves but birds.

The birds burst out of the tree and throw themselves to the ground, all in a matter of seconds, all at once. The tree stands naked again, the birds on the ground and out of her sight. She claps her hands in delight ... even now that she knows the secret, the magic is powerful. She stares at the tree, not daring to look away even for an instant, until, as though through the bewitchment of time's reversal, the leaves that are birds leap backward through the air and clothe the tree in seeming greenery.

And now the tree stands, out of time and out of season.

And now the tree throws off its protection.

And now the tree stands exposed.

And now the tree reaches for cover, pulling shade into its arms.

The same tree.

Every time.

It is summer.

It is fall.

It is winter.

It is spring.

Again.

She glances at the time ... a few minutes still.

She starts the car and drives across the parking lot and along the line of now naked trees, looking for the birds.

When she finds them, they are an ovaled puddle of darkness beneath the tree they have chosen. She mistakes their collective shape at first for the tree's shadow, except that makes no sense and there are no shadows and this shadow seethes with iridescent undulation. The birds are small and dark and glossy, and they work the ground below the tree shoulder to shoulder, wing to wing.

She rolls the car past the birds, and as she passes, the birds fly up into the tree and fill its branches with faux foliage.

Even from this close vantage, the effect is spellbinding.

Just the one tree.

Always the same tree.

Summer, fall, winter, spring.

Again.

She laughs to herself, and for a moment, in the cockeyed rear-view mirror, she sees what her father sees.

She will share this story with her father, and he will not understand. She will share this story of seasons held back and hurried through, of birds that are leaves, of dances performed against muted silver, of surrender and reclaiming, of the alchemy of imagination, of the relinquishment of control. She will speak of winter, of moss footholded within, of the space across which synapses fire being spanned by the falling flight of a feathered shadow. She will speak to him of the sameless, and how it lies not only in the moment but in that moment's perception as well.

Perhaps he will pull her close and whisper into the curtain of her hair, "You died in the winter once. When I was leaving."

"Yes."

She re-parks the car and hurries in.

She hates to be late.

Absence of llama

Eddy stares into the absence. On nights like this, when darkness steals the boundaries of the world, she wonders at the mind's ability to trust. She doesn't believe in much, but isn't that a kind of faith – the belief that morning will arrive after each fall of black? Morning will arrive and with it the world ... a faith rewarded until the particular dawn that doesn't arrive for each of us, one by one.

In the darkness, her thoughts gather her and speak the stories of the time that went before and the time that would come again ... when she was not. Her breath grows ragged against the fabled scrape of truth. Tears bloom against the curves of blind restraint. She doesn't believe in much, but she believes it is going to hurt.

She listens for the depths and scrawls of sleep, matches her breathing to his.

She thinks about waking him, thinks about speaking into the blurred attentiveness that lists between his states of consciousness. There is something about the not-quite of him in those moments she finds reassuring, a certain absorbency to his silence. She imagines her words a pouring, tipped thick upon the sifted earth of him; she imagines in his dreams, he knows her by the visions she nourishes unaware.

Although he claims to never dream, which she chooses to disbelieve.

If she were to speak ...

"Your child won't see the world as you do," the man said, which Eddy had always known, but it hurt, this truth, just the same. She was sitting side by side with her daughter Rhen, who was fifteen, listening to a lecture on parental involvement in teaching one's child to drive. Up to this point, the man had been full of good advice, none of which touched on the particular passenger-seat issue she was having, which was terror.

Eddy supposed the terror went without saying.

Except then he said the terror.

"Your child won't see the world as you do."

It was a simple statement about perspective and experience, a caution for parents that new drivers didn't always know what to look for or how to interpret what they were seeing as they journeyed down the road.

What Eddy heard was a larger truth ... that her perspective died with her, and that nothing – not shared genes or shared history or shared emotion – could make another see the world as she did. Whatever else the man said was lost to panic, and when, some time later, she found herself sitting in the passenger seat as her daughter carefully adjusted the mirrors, Eddy couldn't remember having traveled from her classroom seat to this one. She leaned her head back and closed her eyes, tried to retrieve the last half-hour of her life, but there was nothing.

"You OK, Mom?"

"Yes." She opened her eyes and sat up, stared out the window as Rhen painstakingly backed out of the parking space and navigated the path to the parking lot's exit. "Yes, just a headache."

It was a short ride home through the hills to their house, and she tried very hard not to narrate the intricacies involved in the task of driving, knowing from past experience how much the nervous chatter irritated her daughter. She stared out the window instead, pointing out the beauty of the landscape and the glimmer of the early moon against the darkening blue of the sky and the few stubborn leaves still clinging to the elms. Rhen nodded and grunted acknowledgment but did not turn her head, and even though she knew the girl was focused on the still-novel responsibility of driving the car, Eddy found herself filled with a great sadness.

She sank into silence.

The car crested a slight hill and then dipped to follow the road through a rain-swollen field of untended greenery. Standing in the middle of a muddy patch of grass was a single llama, standing motionless, entirely black. Eddy stared, caught by surprise at the unexpected appearance of the animal, but there was something more ... something about the quality of the black ... a softness of depth to the color that went beyond texture ... or maybe it was the strange way the black stood out against the green in the fading light that needed ...

Rhen interrupted her thoughts, taking a hand briefly off the wheel to point. "Do you see that? It's like the absence of llama."

"What?"

"The black. There's a weird quality to the black. He's standing so still, and his color is so absolute that in this light, it looks as though he is missing." Rhen turned her head to glance at her mother, to be certain she was being understood. "It looks as though there is an empty black blank in the space where a llama should be."

Eddy looked again and whispered, "It is exactly like that."

Rhen continued, "Like he was maybe peeled away. Or maybe he's still in transit, stuck somewhere between there and here, but the scene had to go on without him, and we are in the incompletion."

Eddy wanted to cry. "Yes."

Rhen returned her attention to the road. "I like that thought ... that behind everything there is blackness, and we only get glimpses in the moments of incompletion."

Eddy turned to stare at her daughter, breathless at the thought.

Yes, if she were to speak, she would tell him of the absence of llama.

She lies on her back and closes her eyes against the unseen. Outside the room, the world shifts, and tentative starlight reaches to caress a single side of her face. She lies motionless and unknowing in the incompletion.

Beside her, he stares at the backlit darkness carved of her silhouette.

June

When they were newly married, they bought a house. She spoke into the darkness of having children, and he was quiet. He bought her a puppy.

After a while, over coffee one morning, she spoke again of having children, and when it was his turn to speak, he stared out the window and complained bitterly about the dog shit that littered the back yard. Surprised by his vehemence and wanting him to be happy, she got into the habit of accompanying the dog into the yard whenever it went out. She carried a small roll of plastic bags with her at all times, and the back yard was immaculate.

She brought up children once more, on their third anniversary, and he said simply, "I won't" and then went out to buy plum trees. He spent the afternoon digging four precisely spaced holes in the back yard, and then he planted the trees. She trailed her fingers along the imaginarily perfect square their spindly trunks outlined in the yard ... a smaller yard within the yard.

"Why four?" she asked, "Why not just one tree?"

"I couldn't tell them apart."

"What does that mean?"

"They're dioecious," he said, and he walked away.

She looked it up. It meant that the plants were either male or female; in order to produce fruit, a female tree required a nearby male tree for pollination. Dioecious – Greek for 'of two households.' She asked him, "Do you even like plums?"

He glanced at her. "I read a poem about plums once."

After several years, all four of the trees began to bear fruit, and she wondered how he had even known the word to get it wrong. No one wanted to eat the plums but the dog, and plums made the dog bloated and sick. She still accompanied the dog, whose name was Sam, on every trip into the yard, and so she got into the habit of picking up the fruit as well as the shit. As the weather turned, she raked the fallen leaves. The yard was immaculate.

She preferred the trees in the winter; she felt a kinship with their skeletal dormancy. Sometimes, in the dusk of a day or in the dawn, as she and the dog played, she would be surprised by the scrape of small wooden fingernails against her cheek or across her brow. It occurred to her more than once that she wasn't paying enough attention, that there was an urgency to the tiny scrawls across her flesh that suggested intent.

She satisfied herself with the knowledge that she had noticed she wasn't paying enough attention.

All of this had happened, but most of it was lost to her. She sat now in a different place at a different window and stared out on a different world and pressed a hand softly to her cheek, feeling for the lines she hadn't known to read. She missed Sam, although she was uncertain when she mouthed the longing and heard the whispered sibilance whether Sam had been her husband or the dog.

Sometimes, people appeared and called her June, and that felt wrong and filled with the angry buzz of wasps on fleshy decay.

In the sky outside her window, birds unzipped the dawn from frozen darkness.

Yesterday or a day that was at least not today, she had picked up a small smooth stone, an oblong shape of gray that reminded her of a tiny bundled porcelain infant once at the center of a set of wooden nesting dolls; she did not remember the details of the toy beyond the cracking open of the family's layers ... how the infant lay in darkness until all others were halved. She reached into her pocket now for the reassurance of the stone's slight weight, cupping its form to her fingers, rocking slightly to soothe an unknown ache.

She caressed the stone and waited.

Outside her window stood an oak tree that was not hers except as it obscured what lay beyond its complications. The light of the day grew more resolute, and the branches of the tree were revealed in jumbled stark silhouette against the nothingness of sky. She watched, unworried; within the angles and curves and juxtapositions of patience, they would be revealed.

Like crudely drawn stick-figures carelessly flung from pages into branches, the children appeared, faceless and nameless and hers. A small girl hung from her knees, her hair a cascade of smudged black, her arms waving. A boy stood shyly, his face averted, his shoulders hunched. Another girl stared boldly from an empty oblong. A little boy curled up in the crook of an arm, swaying gently in the breeze. There were hints and suggestions as well ... arms outstretched in embrace, legs flexed in anticipation or stubborn refusal, profiles dipped in nodded agreement and affection.

She swiped at tears and caressed again the memory of long-ago scratches as the children faded into the harsher light of sticks and stones and things broken and halved between houses.

A voice she did not recognize said, "June?" and the room filled with the scent of fruited putrefaction. She steadied herself against the ensuing nausea and slipped the stone into her mouth, her back to the intruder. She cradled the stone on her tongue and raked her fingernails down her cheeks as she watched the last traces of the children fade into the banality of measured time and truth.

Another voice then, and she turned, bleeding and close-mouthed, into the whispered imposition of memories she was certain were not hers.

"Mom?"

She shook her head and swallowed.

Then cracked in half.

First person ... you

Sometimes, when I am doing very badly, I imagine that you hold my hand and say nice things until my breath evens out and my heart calms and my eyes unblur.

In my imagination, you say all the right things.

Thank you for that.

About the author

Kris Wehrmeister lives in Lake Oswego, Oregon with her husband Mark and their two daughters, Maj and Kallan. Rounding out the family are a frog, a turtle, and three dogs. None of them know how to heel.

Kris is a woman of words, and so if there are words you would like to share, feel free to email her at: *kris@prettyalltrue.com*

She will respond, possibly at great length. She has a penchant for the last word and all the words that come before.

If you are interested in more writing from Kris, please check out her offerings at *www.PrettyAllTrue.com*

You can also find her on Twitter at *@PrettyAllTrue* and on Facebook at *Pretty All True.*

Kris is working on her next book, which is filled with laughter.

You'll see.